THE MYSTERIOUS MR WYLIE

WONKY INN BOOK 6

JEANNIE WYCHERLEY

The Mysterious Mr Wylie
Wonky Inn Book 6
by

JEANNIE WYCHERLEY

Bark at the Moon Books

Sign up for Jeannie's newsletter: eepurl.com/cN3Q6L

The Mysterious Mr Wylie was edited by Anna Bloom @ The Indie Hub

Proof Reading by Nikki Groom @The Indie Hub

Cover design by JC Clarke of The Graphics Shed.

Formatting by Tammy

CHAPTER ONE

"Could British Airways passenger Mr W Wylie, travelling on flight BA2472 from Egypt, please proceed to the customer service centre in the luggage hall? Passenger Wylie."

The incessant announcements over the tannoy system swamped my senses. I hadn't been able to drink enough water on my flight, thanks to the silly little plastic cups and disappearing airline hosts, and now I had a headache. The continued insistent announcements, demanding that passengers pay attention, had exacerbated the thumping in my temples. I could really do without it.

Added to this, the straps of my carry-on back-pack were making the sunburn on my shoulders sting like crazy.

Quite frankly, the constant xylophonic bonging preceding each message was enough to drive a witch to distraction. I itched to take my wand out of my pocket and mute the airport's communication system for a few hours.

But that's just not the done thing, is it?

To be fair, I was running a little short on endurance. My flight out of Cairo had been delayed by six hours, and it quickly become apparent that the scratchy feeling at the back of my nose and the fact that my eyes had started to water, meant I was incubating a cold. To add insult to injury—or illness—it had been just my luck that the pilot had missed our landing slot, forcing him to circle the skies above London for an hour and forty minutes. Now, as I stood alongside the baggage carousel, shuffling from one foot to another, I had the sinking sensation that somewhere along the line my main luggage had been lost.

This was tantamount to airline betrayal. I'd followed the herd and had every expectation that things would go to plan.

I'd risen from my seat on the cramped and crowded plane—grateful that I could finally stretch and allow the blood to access my backside for the first time in hours—then trooped dutifully out along with everyone else in search of baggage reclaim. As one we'd stormed along the corridors of Heathrow at a fair clip, part of some strange race to be first to the carousel. Needless to say, our baggage hadn't even made it off the plane. The sole advantage of the delay was that I had plenty of time to visit the bathroom to freshen up, grab a handful of tissues to dab my nose with, and locate a trolley, before listening out for the familiar beep of the carousel starting up.

I hung back, behind everyone else and all their trollies and possessions, to watch the chaotic scene as it unfolded. In my sickly state, my head revolved in its own circle, as bag after bag tumbled out of the dark mouth of the all-powerful machine tasked with reuniting travellers with their dirty laundry.

And I waited.

And I waited.

And I waited some more.

The carousel filled to bursting with impossibly overstuffed holdalls and suitcases. Some had been personalised with gaily coloured luggage straps, but the majority in blue or black looked exactly like a million other bags travelling through Heathrow. How could their owners tell them apart?

I was looking for my green and red rucksack which I'd borrowed from Charity; whose mother Peggy had used it when she'd backpacked around Asia before Charity came along. You'd have thought that given the colours of my bag, it would have stood out a mile.

But no. Not a trace.

After twenty-five long minutes, it became obvious that the bag would never be thrust forth from the black hole of baggage mecca.

I watched, twitching nervily, as a single grey suitcase with a rose decoration near the handle, and a battered brown leather briefcase enjoyed repeated turns on the carousel. Of my gaudy backpack, there was no sign. I sniffled in misery, hoping against hope it would turn up, until it became obvious even to my dulled head, that my luggage had travelled elsewhere without me.

An airport worker ambled along to the conveyor belt, whistling and studiously avoiding my gaze. He pushed a large trolley ahead of himself, loaded with a number of bags and cases. When he spoke into a handheld radio, the baggage carousel shuddered to a stop. He hoisted the grey suitcase with the rose decoration from the belt, scanned its ticket and placed it on his trolley, then he plucked the briefcase from the carousel and repeated the process. He tossed the briefcase, evidently a lightweight item, onto the top of the pile where it balanced precariously.

I decided he looked like a man who knew what

he was doing with lost luggage. It would make sense to ask him about my rucksack.

I shuffled the few steps between us, while he angled himself slightly sideways so that I would be talking to his back. I groaned, an unusually nasal sound that caused me a moment of alarm. *I really am sick*, I thought to myself, longing just to find my coach and head back to Devon. This appeared to be turning into a road trip that would never end.

"Excuse me?" I sidestepped around him so he had to look at me, something he seemed oddly loathe to do. "My bag hasn't arrived. Do you think there will be any more coming out?"

The man sucked his teeth and narrowed his eyes. "I shouldn't have thought so, madam." He pointed with the antennae of his radio at the electronic screen above the baggage carousel displaying my flight number. As if by magick the screen went blank. A microsecond later a new flight code for a plane heading in from Abu Dhabi replaced it.

"Oh." I slumped in disappointment. "What do I do?"

"It's not one of these?" the man asked, indicating the grey suitcase and the briefcase.

Yes. Because I've been standing here like a lemming for the past forty minutes just so that my luggage can enjoy repeated turns on the roundabout. We're all about the fun where I come from.

"No." I forced a smile. "Mine's a rucksack."

"Ah." The man nodded knowingly. "With straps? They can cause a bit of an issue sometimes. They get caught in the machinery." He turned his attention back to his trolley.

I resisted the urge to kick his shins. "What should I do next?"

He nodded towards the side of the arrivals' hall. "Lost luggage."

"Of course. Thanks." I started to turn as he yanked his trolley. The briefcase toppled from the top of the pile and without thinking I reached out to catch it. As it made contact with my hands, I experienced a short thrill, akin to the briefest of electric shocks. It quickly passed. The case was as light as it looked, and nothing rattled inside it. I handed it back to the unhelpful-left-luggage-collecting-official, nodded my thanks, and made a beeline for the customer service desk he'd indicated. Glancing over my shoulder, I thought at first he was following me, but once I'd joined the queue at the desk, I realised he had to manoeuvre his trolley through a large door marked private to the right of the left luggage office. He did so and disappeared from view.

I waited as patiently as I could, my throat dry and scratchy, my eyes tired and stinging. All I wanted in the world was my big comfy bed, in my warm and familiar wonky inn, but those things were hours away.

At least the customer service agents at the left luggage desk were efficient. They rattled through their questions with the two people ahead of me and then it was my turn. A young woman with incredibly tidy hair and immaculate make-up smiled at me from behind her computer screen. Her name, according to her name badge, was Sheronie.

"Good morning, madam. How can I help you today?" Her voice had a pleasant Welsh lilt to it.

"I've lost my rucksack."

"Your luggage hasn't arrived at the carousel?" Sheronie asked, raising an eyebrow as if this were a first, and not something she spent every day of her working life dealing with.

"That's right."

"I'm really sorry to hear that." Her fingers typed something, and she gazed at her screen. "Could I have your passport, flight details and baggage check, please?"

I delved into my little carry-on backpack, experiencing a moment of panic as I looked for the small rectangle of card. I breathed with relief when I located my passport with the details she required tucked alongside my photograph, hidden under soggy tissues.

"Thank you." More frantic typing as Sheronie entered all my details, tapping her keys with a ferocity that seemed to belie her calm exterior.

My attention wandered.

Sheronie and her partner were simply the front-facing partnership of a larger operation. Behind them I could see my lost-luggage pal rescanning his bags and cases and handing them over to someone else. Another woman consulted a handheld machine and began making announcements over the tannoy system.

"Could British Airways passenger Mr W Wylie, travelling with us on flight BA2472 from Egypt, please proceed to the lost luggage customer service centre in the luggage hall? Passenger Wylie."

Wylie?

Why did that name ring a bell?

"What make is your suitcase, Ms Daemonne?" Sheronie interrupted my train of thought.

"It's a rucksack," I repeated. "Erm... gosh... I don't know." I'd been carting the blasted thing around for weeks but hadn't noticed whether it had a brand name or not. “It was green and red.” *Because that would help, surely?*

Sheronie smiled at my wry expression. “Well I don’t suppose there are many of those around.”

I laughed with relief that she hadn’t shrivelled me with a look of professional disdain. “No. I imagine not.”

“And what’s in the rucksack?”

I grimaced. “Mainly my dirty laundry. A few books. Some nick-knacks I’ve picked up on my travels.”

“Nothing valuable?” Sheronie held my gaze. “A camera or anything?”

I shook my head. I’d tried to travel light.

“Great.” Sheronie returned to the keyboard, and I glanced behind her again. The briefcase had been placed on a shelf and attention had turned to the grey suitcase. I looked behind me. There were a few people in the queue. I wondered whether any of them was the owner.

Well lucky them. At least they’d be reunited with their property.

While I waited for Sheronie to input everything she needed, I puzzled over the fact that someone, presumably this Mr Wylie, had checked a briefcase in. Why not carry it on to the plane as hand luggage?

I found that very strange, but there's no accounting for people.

"I think I've located your rucksack, Ms Daemonne. It looks like it's travelled to Charles de Gaulle airport."

"Paris?" *Lucky rucksack!*

"Yes."

I sighed. "What happens now?"

"We'll make sure it travels to London on the next flight out."

"Do I have to wait for it?" I asked, my heart sinking at yet another delay.

Sheronie's smile was reassuring. You couldn't fault her professionalism. "Oh, no no no. We'll have it sent on by courier. It will follow you to your destination. I just need an address."

"Whittle Inn," I started to tell her, the thrill of the words lifting my spirits. "I'm going home to Devon."

Thanks to the numerous delays, it came as no surprise that I'd missed the coach I'd booked onto. Fortunately, after joining yet another queue and having yet another conversation with yet another person stuck behind a computer screen, I was able to swap my ticket for a later coach. I had enough time to grab a cup of tea, a bottle of water, and an over-priced brownie from a nearby café.

Checking my new ticket, I read that I should join stand 'H' and await the arrival of the coach to Penzance, fast to Taunton and then stopping at Exeter and Plymouth before heading into Cornwall. Unable to face yet another queue at the stand, I loitered with intent at the rear of the coach station, my back to the wall, keeping an eye on the buses as they zoomed into my eye line.

It had been such a long day. The only thing keeping me going was nervous tension. While I wanted to get home as quickly as possible of course, I found myself hoping the coach would stop at least once at a motorway services or somewhere, so that I could buy some tissues and some aspirin to try and ward off the worst of my cold. My headache had reached epic proportions.

I kind of felt like I was participating in some kind of TV-reality endurance show, where anything that can go wrong will go wrong, and where the producers throw larger and larger spanners in the works. *I surrender*, I wanted to shout. *I'm a tired witch, get me out of here!*

Another large coach, with 'Manchester' emblazoned on the front panel, swung itself around the corner and into the H bay. Dozens of people swarmed towards it, pushing trollies, or pulling wheelie-cases along after themselves; struggling with heavy baggage. At least I didn't have that to contend with.

With relief I spotted a space on the bench nearest me. I could rest my legs for a few minutes. I carefully slipped into the seat, being very British about not encroaching on the gentleman already sitting there, and rested my small carry-on backpack in my lap. I watched people as they fussed and fretted, jostling in a strangely passive-aggressive way as they climbed on to the coach to claim a seat that they already had a reservation for. Then I zoned out, weary to my bones.

I came back to awareness five minutes later. The Manchester coach beeped loudly as it reversed out of its space, and behind it I could see the Penzance coach waiting patiently to take its place.

At last.

"Excuse me?"

I ignored the voice—who would be talking to me after all? —and took a step towards the throng of people queuing for my coach, pulling my little back-pack over my shoulder.

"Excuse me? Excuse me, love?"

Feeling increasingly vacant, I looked around, just on the off chance someone was trying to grab my attention. An older lady waved at me. "Did you forget your briefcase?"

"Briefcase?" I asked, sounding stupid I'm sure.

She indicated a brown leather briefcase that had been left on the bench next to me. The gentleman had disappeared. I hadn't seen him go.

"No. It's not mine." I frowned, peering around at the people I could see. I wouldn't have remembered the man who'd been sat there even if he was standing in front of me now. I hadn't so much as peeked his face, let alone taken in what he'd been wearing.

I glanced back at the briefcase, very similar to the one that had enjoyed multiple turns around the baggage carousel back in the airport. The same aged-brown leather.

The older woman picked it up. "It feels empty," she said, holding it out to me, as though she hadn't heard me say it wasn't mine.

I took it off her, and once more felt that same quick thrill as I touched it. It *was* the same briefcase after all. It had to be. The woman was right. It held its own weight and nothing else.

The address label attached to the case offered no clues, mainly because there was no address, just the words, 'The Property of Mr W Wylie.'

Wylie again.

Why did I recognise that name?

"It's not mine," I repeated. "It needs to go to lost property." But I was talking to thin air. The old woman had disappeared.

"Argh," I growled in frustration. How did I have the time to take this to the customer service desk now? My coach had pulled in and started boarding passengers. I didn't want to miss my ride home again.

Without looking around, apprehensive of drawing attention to myself, I quickly flicked at the clasps holding the case closed. It hadn't been locked. Now I flipped it open and revealed... precisely nothing. As I'd suspected, the briefcase was empty.

But there was something about it that nagged at me. That little tingle when I touched it. This was no ordinary briefcase. There had to be magick involved somewhere.

Without further ado I reached into the pocket of my robes and plucked out my wand, my little piece of Vance from the marshes back home. "*Revelare!*" I demanded.

I wasn't even slightly surprised to find the case suddenly stuffed full of a motley collection of bizarre items. A stuffed rat, a clock, some charts, a brass telescope, a barometer, several heavily annotated notepads, a bag of beads and a few jars of what looked like glitter.

The briefcase belonged to a wizard, and now I remembered *exactly* where I'd come across that name before.

Chapter Two

Have you ever been so tired that you wanted to crawl on your hands and knees to the nearest soft warm place, and then just curl up and pass out? That's exactly how I felt when my taxi pulled up in front of Whittle Inn at just before 2.30 a.m. I'd been travelling for twenty hours and my cold was now making itself fully known.

I paid the taxi driver and turned to gaze at my beloved wonky inn. It stared down at me, all crooked walls and kinked turrets. Lights burned in a few of the bedroom windows, just as I expected. Many of our guests were nocturnal creatures.

'Creature' being the operative word in many cases.

I somehow found the energy to let myself in through the front door. The bar area was deserted, but that was okay. I didn't want to disturb anyone.

I tiptoed through the bar and into the back passage, popping my head around the kitchen door. No sign of Florence. Boo! I'd been looking forward to seeing her again.

I carried on up the stairs and into my bedroom. My big bed with its soft downy quilt and clean linen looked like paradise. Like everyone else, Mr Hoo, my owl, was nowhere to be seen either, but I figured he'd be out hunting.

I yanked off my robes, tossing them into the corner, and then dragged myself into the bathroom to scrub my hands and face and brush my teeth. I desperately needed a shower, but I figured that could wait till morning.

I had just clambered into bed and was reaching to turn off my sidelight when my long-dead great-grandmother appeared. I blinked sleepily at her apparition.

"Welcome home, Alfhild," she said in her well-modulated tone. She always liked to call me by my formally given name. I'd been named after her. She was Alfhild Gwynfyre, a Daemonne by marriage. I secretly referred to her as Gwyn, but not to her face. "I trust you had a pleasant trip."

"Oh, it was wonderful!" I gushed. "I have so

much to tell you." I thumped my pillow. "But right now? Now I'm exhausted. And I don't feel well."

Gwyn floated a little closer and regarded me in what I decided was concern but might have been scepticism given what she said next.

"I do hope you haven't brought home some sort of foreign disease, dear child."

Child? I was thirty-one! "It's a cold, Grandmama."

"It's not Spanish influenza is it? That killed over fifty million people in 1918, you know?"

I shook my head. I didn't know that. Goodness me. Imagine the sheer number of ghosts that had spawned. "Thank goodness they didn't all end up here," I murmured.

"Pardon?" Gwyn asked sharply.

"Nothing, Grandmama. Don't worry. It's a cold. Not the flu." I looked at her pointedly. "I haven't been to Spain. I just need some sleep."

Gwyn sniffed. Had I hurt her feelings? Ghosts don't need sleep. She could probably have chatted all night.

"I'll share all my adventures with you in the morning," I promised.

"After a good long bath, I hope. Soak the smell of the souk away."

I gaped at her in disbelief. Since when had ghosts had any sense of smell? I shook my head at her. "Night, Grandmama." I switched the light off.

Her glow remained in place, as I drifted off to sleep. "Good to have you home, my dear," I thought I heard her say. I sighed with satisfaction and knew no more.

A light scratching on the cover near my face woke me the next morning. I lay where I was, my eyes closed tightly, my head pounding. Were they digging up the cellar again? Or maybe filling it in? Hadn't that work been completed yet? I'd left instructions...

But it was just the throbbing of a headache. My throat and sinuses ached in sympathy.

The scratching came again. My eyes flicked reluctantly open. Mr Hoo had landed on the bedcovers, and now his talons pricked at the material as he lifted up first one foot and then the other, stamping about as though he just didn't care.

"Hello, adorable!" I grinned at him and reached out to gently stroke his chest. He ducked his head and pecked gently at my fingers. "I've missed you lots!" My voice was thick, my sinuses completely bunged up. The calm before the storm, no doubt. As soon as I sat up, I'd be streaming.

"Where's that Florence?" I asked my owl. "I thought she'd have been to see me by now."

"Hooooo?" he called. "Hooo?"

"You know full well who." I pushed myself up to sitting.

I called for her myself, "Florence?" but she didn't appear. Perhaps everyone was busy downstairs dealing with the breakfast service.

"My head aches," I told Mr Hoo. "And I'm still so tired." I snuggled back down beneath the covers. "Maybe I need a pre-breakfast nap." I closed my eyes and heard him flutter on to the bedstead where he liked to perch. "Just a little more sleep," I mumbled.

It seemed like only seconds later that I heard a knock on the door. "Hello?" I called, my voice husky.

The door cracked open and Charity poked her head around it. She beamed when she spotted me. "Yes! You're home!" She pushed the door open wide and came into the room, carrying a tray. "Gwyn said you weren't feeling very well."

"It's just a cold." I sat up once more and arranged my pillows more comfortably.

"Travelling kills the immune system." Charity nodded. "It's all that recycled air in planes."

"Eww." I twisted my nose up at that idea. "It's so nice to be home. You're a sight for sore eyes."

"As are you. Oh! I'm so pleased to have you back. We've all missed you."

I wondered for a moment whom Charity meant by 'all'. She looked at me knowingly and I rolled my eyes.

"It's been great to get away from everything," I said firmly. "But yes, it is fantastic to be back. You have to fill me in on all that's been happening here."

Charity placed the tray on my thighs. A bowl of Greek yoghurt with fresh peach slices, dribbled with honey. Two slices of toast. A small pot of tea with milk in a jug. And a packet of aspirin.

"Perfect," I announced, and poured a test amount of tea into the cup. It needed a good stir.

Charity sat down on the bed and watched me. "George has been asking after you," she said, subtle as a sledgehammer.

"Has he?" I asked carefully.

Before I'd departed Whittle Inn for foreign shores, I'd returned to the marsh to relieve my erstwhile fiancé of the spell I'd cast on him after I'd found he'd been playing away from home. To be fair, I truly believed that his involvement with Stacey, the girl from the local emergency police call centre, was little more than a flirtation. She had obviously been keen on him for some time. The thing is, as my mother would have said, it takes two to tango. I could forgive him—them—for their harmless dalliance, but I'd done some soul-searching of my own, and I wasn't sure that George and I should proceed with our engagement until we both felt it was the right thing to do.

"He misses you." Charity's tone wheedled away at me.

"I missed him, too." But really I had missed 'us'. Now I couldn't be sure there even was an us. I was reminded of something someone had said to me not so long ago. '*Love makes you weak. It's the thin end of a wedge that can be used to crack open the door before bludgeoning you to death.*'

That had been Silvan. My annoying dark witch friend.

"Have you heard from Silvan?" I asked.

Charity pouted, sour because I'd changed the subject. "No. Not since he disappeared back to London."

I poured my tea, this time happy with the colour. "Has everything been okay while I've been gone? No sign of 'our friends'?"

Charity knew that 'our friends' was the

euphemism we used when we were talking about my arch-enemies, The Mori. The Mori were a secretive band of nasty warlocks, hell bent on taking my land away from me by whatever means they could. A few months ago, we'd had a showdown that had resulted in the death of their regional leader. We had sent the rest of them scurrying away, their tails between their legs.

"We've had no new problems at all." Charity nodded at the window, knowing what I was going to ask next. "The perimeter is safe and secure. Finbarr checks it every day. And there are still a couple of your dad's friends hanging out in the wood."

Finbarr was an Irish witch who seemed to have made Whittle Inn his permanent home. He was a huge help and I thought of him as my annoying younger brother. He liked to perform magick using his band of pixies. To define the rotten knee-high, pointy-eared little creatures as a menace was an understatement.

But it could have been worse. At least they weren't leprechauns.

"But not my dad?" I sighed. It wasn't really a question so much as a statement. I didn't see a huge amount of my father. As a member of the Circle of Querkus, he was sworn to track down and eliminate The Mori, and that meant he spent little time here at the inn. Like my great-grandmother, Erik was a ghost, but it was good to have them both around.

"Never mind." Charity patted my hand. "You've still got us."

In this instance 'us' referred most specifically to Zephaniah, Monsieur Emietter, Ned and Florence – my house ghosts. "But where *is* Florence?" I asked, puzzled. "I haven't seen her since I arrived home. That's unusual for her." Florence loved to mind my business.

Charity pulled a face. "Florence has a new interest."

"What sort of interest?" I asked as I tucked into my delicious yogurt and peaches.

Her reply was a grunt. "Huh. You'll see."

Despite how groggy and spent I felt with the residue tiredness from all the travelling and the first stage of my cold, I kept fairly busy all day. My rucksack, delivered by an airport courier, arrived at the inn after lunch. I handed out gifts to Charity and Finbarr and held court in the kitchen over copious amounts of lemon tea, regaling everyone with my foreign adventures.

Of Florence there remained no sign.

At around five, I left everyone else to prepare for the dinner service. We'd decided that I shouldn't help that evening as I'd only end up spreading my germs. I elected instead to make my way to my office and take stock on what had been happening in my absence.

Charity had stayed on top of all the inn's business just as I'd expected she would. There were a few outstanding reservations to process, but apart from that everything appeared up-to-date. I checked the finances and things were looking as healthy as they could, given the enormous amount of money I'd forked out to have the hole in the cellar filled in. That and the cost of having two of my cottages in Whittlecombe double-glazed, painted externally and re-roofed caused me to wince in pain whenever I looked at the figures involved.

But things could have been worse. In fact, I'd expected there to be a larger deficit. Scrolling back through the bank statements I noticed one glaring omission. The cheque I'd given to Silvan as a final payment for services rendered had never been cashed. I double checked, then triple checked.

Why hadn't he cashed it?

Silvan was a rogue, a dastardly dark witch. He loved money and a good fight and not much else. I found it strange that he hadn't cashed my cheque. I made a mental note to ringfence the money in my business account so it wouldn't be spent. I could try and contact Silvan to see if he was alright too, although I knew from experience that might be easier said than done.

I scribbled a note to myself on a post-it note, and as I did so I remembered the briefcase from the airport. I'd realised at the bus station where I'd heard the name Mr Wylie. Right here at the inn. Now I wanted to check his registration details. A quick search by name yielded no results in my database so I had a look at the planner I liked to keep in my desk drawer with all my scribblings in. Checking out the date of the Psychic Fayre, way back in April—which felt like a lifetime ago—I worked out the date that a Mr Wylie had stayed at Whittle Inn.

From there it should have been a simple case of looking back through the bookings at that time and cross-referencing. But no matter which way I looked at the notes, by date or name or room, I could find no record of the mysterious Mr Wylie.

He had been erased from the inn's records.

Gwyn chose that moment to float along the corridor outside the office.

"Grandmama?"

I thought I sensed a little reluctance as my great-grandmother turned about and drifted into the office. "Yes, dear?"

"You remember Mr Wylie who stayed here in April while I was... camping out at the Psychic Fayre?" I looked up at her expectantly.

"No, dear."

"No?"

"No."

I sat back in my seat and frowned at her. "No, you don't remember Mr Wylie? Or you don't remember the date...? Or you don't remember the Fayre?"

"Well, of course, I remember the time you impersonated a fortune teller, my dear. Who could forget that absurd get-up? But I never had cause to visit the Fayre, so I don't remember it *per se*. I recall that it occurred. Will that suffice?"

I tutted. She could be such a pedantic old ghost. "But Mr Wylie? You remember him?"

"I can't say I do. Is there a problem?"

Taken aback, I frowned at her. Gwyn was as sharp as a tack. She never forgot anything. "He stayed here a few nights while I was away," I explained slowly, watching her face as I did so. "He claimed he was a businessman."

Gwyn shrugged her shoulders. An impressive gesture in someone as grandly dressed—in a long velvet evening gown and a tiara—as she was. "No. Nothing's coming back to me."

She was lying. I was sure of it. I held her gaze, and she met mine without blinking.

"Florence was concerned about him." Why was she being so evasive?

Gwyn turned about, creating a draft around the desk and making the papers in front of me rustle. "I suggest you ask her then."

"I would," I began to answer but Gwyn had disappeared, slipping like smoke down a crack in the floorboards. "Except I haven't seen her since I arrived home," I finished to myself. It sounded lame.

I returned my attention to the computer, running another check for the name W Wylie and finding nothing. I couldn't help feeling disappointed in Gwyn.

It was so unlike her not to tell it to me straight. I could only assume that something somewhere was seriously wrong.

I sneezed and the throbbing in my head started up again.

I loved this inn and everyone in it, so why couldn't anything be straightforward? Yet again I had something I needed to get to the bottom of.

The sooner the better.

Chapter Three

"Hey, boss." Charity poked her head around the door of my office the next morning after breakfast. "How's your cold?"

"I'b combletely blogg'd ub," I replied, laying it on a little thick and waving a wad of tissues around.

"Lemon and whisky, that's what my Mum always recommends." Charity swished into the room, full of sass and energy, her hair dyed a flame red, which was fitting for late summer.

"Good old Mum," I said, tidying up the chaos on my desk. "I'm not a big whisky drinker though. I'll just stick to lemon and ginger, I think."

"Maybe some air would do you good? You haven't been out since you came back."

"It's only been a couple of days and I'm poorly." I tried—and probably succeeded—in sounding pathetic. "Don't you feel sorry for me?"

"No. It's only a cold." Charity chuckled. "It's not even man flu. You need to get over yourself."

I folded my arms and gave her a baleful stare. "It's worse than man flu, it's witch flu!"

"Heaven help me. You do go on." We laughed together and Charity skipped over to the window to glance outside. "They're promising rain later, but it's only a little overcast at the moment. A walk would do you good."

"Are you trying to get rid of me?" I joined her at the window, but she backed away, crossing her fingers into the age-old 'unclean' gesture.

"I am as it happens. The post office rang."

"From the village?"

"Yep. They've had a delivery that they think may or may not be for us."

What did that mean? "Well is it for us? Or isn't it?"

Charity shrugged. "I don't know. They want someone, preferably you, to go and have a look at it. It doesn't have a return address so they can't tell us who it's from."

Weird.

"Well, alright then. I'll have a little stroll down to the village. It'll be nice to catch up with everyone."

"Just don't go spreading your germs around. We

don't want the whole village catching 'witch' flu." Charity smirked at me. "You know what happens when the village gets sick."

"Don't remind me," I grumbled. "I'll wear a mask."

I didn't go that far of course. The day was cool, Autumn on the horizon once more, but I didn't require a coat. I enjoyed the walk despite feeling a little lightheaded and spaced out. The trees were at their most bounteous and green, dancing in the breeze above my head. The cottage gardens I passed by were full of roses and late summer flowers. Fat, lazy bees buzzed among the blooms, while slender and slightly more determined wasps darted at me with deadly intent.

Yes, it was *that* time of year.

I swatted the wasps away, but when they kept coming back I decided to take shelter in Millicent's cottage. I let myself in through her tiny front gate and slipped sideways among the rose bushes to knock at her door. Instant barking greeted me and Millicent, dressed eccentrically as always in some sort of navy blue crocheted-jumpsuit monstrosity teamed with a bright orange blouse, flung her door open wide and reached out to hug me.

"Alf! You're home! So lovely to see you!"

What a welcome. Jasper, Millicent's scruffy lurcher, and Sunny, her adopted Yorkshire Terrier, danced around my legs excitedly. Jasper burrowed his nose between my knees while Sunny jumped up to lick my hands—or bite my fingers depending on your perspective.

"Don't hug me," I said quickly. "I've come home with a lurgy."

"Oh, poor you," Millicent sympathised with me quite rightly, and with what I considered to be the proper degree of care and concern. "Well come in anyway and let me see what I can fix you."

I hoped there would be cake or at least biscuits. Florence's continuing and perplexing absence might do wonders for my waistline, but I was suffering from a serious sugar withdrawal.

I followed Millicent into the tiny kitchen and watched as she filled her kettle. "Thanks for the post-cards," she said, indicating the fridge where she'd stuck all three. "It looks like you had a fantastic time."

"I had some very interesting adventures," I

agreed. "I really must travel more. The people you meet can be extraordinary."

Millicent smiled. "More interesting that the ones you come across in Whittlecombe you mean?"

I pulled a face in response. "Nowhere is more interesting than Whittlecombe."

"Not after the year you've had anyway. It must have been good to get away."

"It was the right thing to do." Whenever I thought of George, my heart hurt a little bit. I would have to get in touch with him and see how the land was lying. I watched as Millicent rummaged in one of her lower cupboards, listening to the chink of glass as she moved jars around.

"Where is it?" she was saying, bending down, her head buried.

"What are you looking for?" It wouldn't be cake. Not in that cupboard.

Millicent's voice travelled to me as if from a deep cave. "Hang on a sec." She drew back. "Ooh. It's been a while since I sorted this lot out, but here we are." She sat back on her haunches and twisted at the waist to face me, brandishing a half pint bottle of vibrant purple liquid. A pretty dried flower decoration had been tied around the neck with a faded lilac ribbon.

"What's that?" I asked, trying not to sound too dubious as I reached for it.

Millicent stood and brushed herself down. "It's my blackberry cordial. It's from a very old recipe that my grandmother taught me."

I studied the bottle. As clear as glass, there was no sediment in the purple liquid. It sparkled in the light. The decoration was lavender. It gave off a faint fragrance. "Blackberry doesn't sound too bad. It's good for colds, is it?"

"This potion is the best cure for colds there is. Trust me."

"Great. Thanks."

Millicent ran the water in the sink so she could wash her hands. "Of course, it's not just blackberry. There's a little lavender in there. A little damson wine."

That still sounded fairly innocuous. Pleasant even.

"A smidge of deadly nightshade and the filings of a black rat's claw," Millicent continued.

Oh.

"And skin shavings from a plague victim's cadaver."

I placed the jar down on Millicent's countertop and backed away. "Seriously?"

Millicent cackled with evil glee and wiped her hands dry. "Not the latter, silly. But yes to the deadly nightshade and the rat's claw. Our ancestors used to believe that all coughs and colds were related to the plague. So, they practised an early form of inoculation by incorporating symbolic elements within their potions. What doesn't kill you..."

"Makes you better." I sniffed. "Hmmm."

"I promise that this will make you feel well in no time."

"Alright." I could trust her, she was my friend after all.

"Go through to the lounge. I'll bring through the tea."

"Will there be biscuits?" I asked, ever hopeful.

Millicent shooed me away. "I'll see what I can do."

I had to borrow a carrier bag from Millicent as I hadn't thought to bring one, and she had loaded me up with some jam and chutney to take back to the inn in addition to her interesting cold remedy. I clinked as I walked through the door of the musty smelling post office. We had a very small post office in the village next to Whittlecombe's General Stores. They sold stationery and cards and other bits and bobs that helped to supplement their income, but I had no idea how they carried on making a living. So many small village post offices had been closed over the years, we were lucky to still have ours. I guess it helped that Whittle Estate—otherwise known as me—only charged them a peppercorn rent.

I'd wager this place hadn't changed much in nearly one hundred and fifty years. All of the wood was original, the shelving and the counter. The only new item appeared to be the glass that had been added to the counter as a security precaution.

"Good afternoon." Beatrice Grey, the small owl-faced woman behind the counter looked up from what she was doing and nodded at me. She ran the post office with her husband Gordon, a man as tall and broad as she was short and thin. He was nowhere in sight today though.

"Afternoon," I replied with a smile. "I believe you have a parcel for me?"

Beatrice placed her pen carefully down on a ledger in front of her and regarded me with a great deal of solemnity. "Well... that's not strictly true."

Was I here on false pretences? "Oh?"

"It's all very irregular, Ms Daemonne. Let me

show you." She bent to take a look under her counter and then drew out a fair-sized parcel. Obviously a box, it had been wrapped in brown paper and measured perhaps, 60 centimetres by 40 centimetres with a depth of 25 centimetres or so. The name and delivery address had been written with artistic flair in bright green ink.

Mrs Alfhild Gwynfyre Daemonne

c/o The Post Office

Whittlecombe

Devon

UK

Earth

Earth?

"You see the problem?" Beatrice's quiet voice broke into my thoughts.

"It's addressed to my great-grandmother," I said, taken aback by the sudden realisation.

"Exactly." Beatrice sounded triumphant. "You see why we couldn't simply deliver it to you at the inn? We needed to know you would accept delivery."

"Yes, of course I will." I nodded, flipping the parcel over to examine the reverse. As Charity had said there was no return address and no indication where the parcel had come from. "Why would someone send anything to my great-grandmother?" I wondered aloud.

Beatrice nodded, her face shining at the mystery of it all. "Especially when she's been dead... what? Fifty years?"

"Oh... and the rest... More like seventy I think." I took the box from Beatrice. Finding it wasn't so heavy that I couldn't carry it home, I gave it a gentle shake. There was something sizeable inside.

"Well I suppose given that you are her heir, you are entitled to take her mail. Regardless of what it is and however long it has been held up in the system..."

I examined the stamps. There were a number of them. Some of them appeared positively vintage. I didn't recognise any of them as current. "Are these stamps all British?" I asked Beatrice.

She slipped a pair of spectacles onto the bridge of her nose and took a closer look. "Hmm. Yes. Yes, they are. How interesting, Ms Daemonne. There are some real classics here." She ran her finger over one of them. "There's one here from The Festival of Britain. 1951. Very nice. Oh, and look." She pointed out another one. "British trees. I remember these. There were several editions over a couple of years. Early to mid-seventies. And here... this British Army one? That's The Royal Welch Fusiliers from 1983, I believe. I could look them up if you're interested."

"Has this parcel been lost somewhere?" I was confused as to the date it had been sent. Gwyn had already been dead twenty years by the time the tree stamps had been issued.

Beatrice shrugged. "I'm sorry, I can't help you there. I found it on the step when I opened. It didn't come with the regular delivery."

"And it's legal to send a parcel with old stamps on it?"

"Yes. They can be used regardless of how long you've had them. They just need to be combined to make up the value of postage required."

"So, this has the correct postage for today?"

"Yes."

Curiouser and curiouser.

"Will you sign for it, Ms Daemonne?" Beatrice reached behind the counter for a little handheld device and I made a wiggly signature using my finger on the screen. Everything is digitalised these days, I mused, reminded of the worker at the airport who had scanned the baggage on the carousel. "All done!" Beatrice returned the device to its place. "Let me know if you want us to look at the stamps for you. Gordon is a keen philatelist."

"I will do," I promised and bid her a good afternoon.

There was a sleepy air over the inn when I returned. The heavy sky, promising rain imminently, had put a downer on some of my guests' activities. My father had started a craze for games on the lawn—croquet and tennis, giant chess and cricket chief among those —and my guests had always gone wild for them. Witches, wizards, sages, mages, ghosts, goblins and the occasional Fae (but never vampires) had proved time and time again to be the biggest children at heart.

But of course, these could only be played when the weather was fine. I'd invested in a cupboard full of board games for wet weather but on dreary afternoons like today, when ostensibly the weather should still have been warm enough to enjoy the outdoors, people couldn't help but feel cheated.

I noticed the bar lacked a little atmosphere this afternoon and it occurred to me this was because the fire had not been lit. The fires were Florence's main job.

I dumped the parcel on the counter in the

kitchen, along with Millicent's jars of preserves and the blackberry potion and went in search of my missing housekeeper. I searched all her known 'haunts', primarily the attic rooms, and eventually located her in one of the small back guest bedrooms. She was splayed out on an unmade bed, staring at the wall.

Well, not really the wall. The guest who had last inhabited this room had obviously requested the use of a television. As a general rule Whittle Inn did not provide televisions or other electronic equipment in guest bedrooms unless it had been specifically requested.

"Florence?" I poked my head around the bedroom door. The room smelt quite strongly of smoke. Poor Florence had lost her life while laying a fire in the bar during the 1880s and her smouldering ghost had haunted the inn ever since. Fortunately for the guests, her face, while permanently covered in soot, had been spared any serious burns.

I waved the stench away and strode across the room to fling the curtains wide and open the window. "Florence!"

My housekeeper looked up at me from where she lay, blinking in bemusement. "Miss Alf? I didn't know you were home."

"Evidently." I regarded her astutely. "I've been back a few days now."

Florence jumped up. "I'm so sorry, Miss Alf. The time just runs away with me." Her eyes darted back to the television set.

I followed her gaze. What on earth was she watching? On the screen, a woman with pink hair was cutting out tiny tubes of what looked like banana-coloured plasticine. As the camera panned out, I realised that the plasticine was actually marzipan or some sort of edible icing. The woman was a baker creating a cake decorated with approximately one zillion teeny-weeny hedgehogs. The tubes would form the face and underbody of the hedgehog, and tiny chocolate shards would become the prickles.

The detail was intricate, and I watched entranced as the baker lady worked quickly and efficiently to insert the spikes into the body.

"Wow," I said, perching on the edge of the bed. "If I tried that the chocolate would melt in my fingers before it got anywhere near the body. How is she going to get each of those little hedgehogs to stick to the side of the cake?"

"That's the really clever bit, Miss Alf." Florence

sat back down next to me. "And you should see what she can do with flamingos."

It was over two hours before I made it down to the kitchen again. It transpired that Florence, who had never previously had occasion to watch television, had become addicted to Witchflix. More specifically to the cooking and bakery shows. I'd sat with her and watched back-to-back episodes of *The Great Witchy Cake-Off.* Turned out these shows were as addictive as the sugary treats the contestants produced. If I hadn't forced Florence to surrender control of the remote, I'd have ended up watching a whole season's worth of *Bake Wars,* sitting alongside her and drooling with desire.

Enough was enough. It had to be.

"Everything in moderation," I'd suggested to my now-slightly grumpy housekeeper. "The inn and our guests have to come first. There's nothing wrong with you having a little down time when there's nothing else to do."

She'd acquiesced. Florence was generally good-natured, and I couldn't help feeling a little guilty. Ghosts don't need sleep, but maybe I was working her too hard? An eternity of cleaning Whittle Inn wasn't the most exciting afterlife, after all.

The parcel was exactly where I'd left it. Monsieur Emietter was working around it, chopping vegetables and simmering stock for this evening's meals. I smiled at him in apology for getting in his way, but he simply glared at me as I removed the package. "It's for Gwyn," I explained, as though that would earn me his forgiveness. "Have you seen her?"

Monsieur Emietter gestured at me to leave his kitchen. Knives flew through the air to hack at herbs that hung above my head. My spirit chef didn't speak a word of English, but he was by far the best chef in the business.

And his aim was deadly.

I took the hint and carried the parcel out of the busy kitchen and up the stairs to the office. "Gwyn?" I called as I entered, finding Charity already in situ, a pen between her teeth as she pored over the computer.

Gwyn apparated into the room. "You called me, my dear?"

"Why didn't either of you tell me about Florence's newfound obsession with the TV?" I asked.

Charity shrugged. "I didn't want you to be cross with her."

"I'm not cross," I confirmed. "I just find it rather odd." Did they think I was excessively bad-tempered? Surely not I?

Charity giggled. "It's just the baking shows really."

"And that one with the witches," Gwyn chipped in. "The new drama series. All these teenage witches performing perfect magick. It's absolute codswallop of course, but she seems to like it."

I couldn't believe what I was hearing. "Have you been watching too?"

"When it's on," my great-grandmother replied airily. "It passes the time. I could give them some pointers about witchcraft though."

I shook my head in disbelief. I could just imagine Gwyn turning up at the production office to put them right about their portrayal of witches in a fantasy television drama. "I'm sure the producers would appreciate it, Grandmama."

"Perhaps I'll write to them," she replied. "And make some suggestions for future improvements."

That reminded me. "Have you been ordering things, Grandmama? From a catalogue or... dare I say it... the Internet?"

Gwyn frowned at me. "Ordering things? Whatever do you mean?"

I picked up the parcel and showed her. "This came to the post office. But it's addressed to you, not me."

Gwyn floated over to stand next to me and peer down at the writing. "Who is it from?"

"Unknown. I'll have to open it."

Gwyn nodded. "Well go ahead, my dear." Ghosts can interact with the physical world by using energy, almost by telekinesis. It's the same energy that helps a poltergeist—or a bad-tempered shouty spirit—throw things around the room. My great-grandmother could have opened the parcel if she wanted to, but it was easier for me to do so on her behalf.

Charity made a little more space at the desk. I placed the parcel back down, and then carefully slit the string that had been tied around it, followed by the Sellotape. The paper quickly fell away and revealed a plain brown cardboard box. Again, there was nothing written on it, nothing stuck to it, nothing that gave us a clue as to the contents of the box or who had sent it. The Sellotape used to secure the lid of the box was old. So old it had lost its stickiness. I reached to peel it back and it slipped away from my fingers.

"Wait," Gwyn commanded, and I moved away.

She gestured, just a small movement, and the lid of the box lifted of its own accord to reveal an item covered with faded tissue paper. Another small movement of her fingers and the tissue paper had slipped sideways.

To reveal a briefcase.

But not a briefcase. *The* briefcase.

"What on this good green earth—" I began but Gwyn's reaction was extraordinary. She retreated backwards, across the room to the window, quickly, as though she had been shot. Charity looked on; her eyes wide.

"What's up?" she asked. "Who's sending Gwyn a briefcase?"

"That's what I want to know, too." I turned to my great-grandmother. "Grandmama?"

Gwyn folded her arms across her not insubstantial bosom. "I have no idea. Is there a note with it?"

I knew there wouldn't be, but I reached into the box and lifted the briefcase free of its wrappings. The familiar battered brown leather mocked me. I'd ignored it at the luggage carousel, but it had been persistent. It had followed me to the coach station.

I'd handed it over to a passing member of staff and thought I'd seen the last of it.

But no. Like a bad penny it had turned up on my doorstep.

Addressed to my great-grandmother. The greatest witch of her generation.

And the briefcase belonged to one of our kind.

That couldn't be a coincidence.

"There's no note." I'd known there wouldn't be.

"What's inside?" Charity asked. "Anything?

"Open it," I said without taking my eyes from Gwyn.

Charity did as I asked. She flicked the catches and then eased the lid up. To all intents and purposes the briefcase was empty. I reached into my robes and took out my wand.

"No." Gwyn said, so softly I doubt Charity heard her, but the word floated across the room, a feather on the gentlest of breezes. I hesitated, my hand in mid-air.

"The property of W Wylie?" Charity had found the little address tag attached to the handle. "That name rings a bell..."

"Does it?" I asked, frowning at Gwyn, willing her to come clean.

"Not with me," Gwyn lifted her chin and glared at me.

"I think you'll find he stayed here at the inn when I was down at the Psychic Fayre being fabulous if you recall." I reminded Charity.

She nodded. "Oh, that's right. A quiet man. Didn't really mix with the other guests. He stayed a few nights." She turned back to the keyboard. "Well I'll be able to pull his records up from here, and we can reunite him with his briefcase."

I shook my head and lifted my wand. "You won't find any details because for some reason they've been wiped off the record."

"He was a businessman, wasn't he?" Charity tapped away. "That's right. He said he'd tried to get a room at *The Hay Loft*, but they were full," she chirruped on, unaware of the tension building between Gwyn and myself. "I don't think he liked being at the inn with all of our super-natural guests. It must have been a bit strange for him."

Gwyn moved towards me like lightning. "Just leave it, Alfhild."

I ignored her. "*Revelare*!" I tapped my wand against the briefcase and once more it filled up with all the paraphernalia our mysterious Mr Wylie had mislaid.

Charity gawped at the contents of the case. "Where did they come from? What is all this stuff?" She poked around among the small glittery jars, the charts and notebooks, the telescope, the watch and so on. "Who carries this kind of stuff?"

"A wizard," I said. "And one whom—for some reason—wants us to hold on to his briefcase."

"But why?" Charity asked, confused. "Is he coming to stay again. Will he want to claim it back? What are we supposed to do with it?"

All good questions. I looked at Gwyn to see whether she could shed some light with a few answers, but she was already apparating away.

And where she goes, nobody knows.

CHAPTER FOUR

I accomplished something incredibly brave.

Yes, I managed to drink a small glass of Millicent's blackberry potion before I went to bed, and lo and behold, it actually worked. I suppose I shouldn't have been surprised, but at that stage of my cold I would have expected a runny nose and sneezes for another few days followed by a week of blocked sinuses.

The following morning, I woke up and felt almost normal. Or what passes for normal in my life.

I repeated the process the next night and woke with more zing in my step than I'd had since arriving back into the UK. With all that extra energy I tackled some jobs that needed sorting around the inn with gusto.

I arranged a breakfast meeting with everyone concerned—Charity, Zephaniah, Ned, Monsieur

Emietter who wouldn't understand a word I would say, Florence (torn away from her beloved baking shows once more) and Gwyn. Gwyn had been keeping her distance from me, but seeing as I hadn't mentioned the briefcase again, perhaps she was softening a little. She turned up to listen to what I had to say at least.

"I've inspected the cellar," I said to my gathering of oddities, "and I'm really pleased with the work that's taken place down there to cover the well and fix the floor. We obviously found a diamond of a building contractor, so I think I'd like to keep them on." I smiled around at everyone. "We've done such a great job of building up a clientele for the inn, and everything looks wonderful, so I'd like to move on to the next phase."

I shuffled the papers I'd brought down from the office. "These are a few plans that I've had drawn up. I think it's time we dragged this wonky inn into the twenty-first century—"

There were some collective murmurings, and I held up my hands. "Don't fret. Nothing major. We're not going to paint everything beige or put in glass partition walls or anything. I just want to remodel some bedrooms so they have their own en-suite."

We had several dozen bedrooms and some of

them had to either share a bathroom or they had a bathroom that wasn't connected. All the bathrooms in the inn were original, with large claw foot baths and institutional cracked wall tiles. I figured all that old décor could stay. They added to the character of the place.

"It's a fairly simple undertaking," I continued. "It will just involve putting new doors in where previously there haven't been any and bricking up the old doors and redecorating. Nothing too major."

Charity nodded enthusiastically. "That sounds like a good idea to me. The separate bathrooms don't bother most of our guests the way they might at *The Hay Loft*, but en-suites are definitely something that the younger generation prefer. I say go for it."

"Excellent." I looked around at everyone else. Monsieur Emietter was studying a carrot with malevolent intent, everyone else seemed to be on board.

Apart from Gwyn.

Her eyes studied me with a sharp intensity. "Which rooms are you talking about?"

I cocked my head in puzzlement, taken aback by her vitriolic tone. "*The Throne Room* and *Neverwhere* to begin with."

She pursed her lips. "I don't think it's a good idea."

"Why not?" I demanded. "It won't hurt the fabric or feel of the inn."

"The guests are happy enough. We have so many who come back time and time again." She had a point, but I didn't think the changes I'd proposed would make the inn any worse or change the experience in any tangible way.

Gwyn's recalcitrance didn't worry me overly much. She was from a much older generation who weren't accustomed to new-fangled ideas like en-suite bathrooms and central heating and the like.

"Grandmama," I said gently. "You worry too much."

"You shouldn't mess with what doesn't concern you, Alfhild," my great-grandmother told me, somewhat cryptically.

"It concerns us all." I indicated everyone around us. "That's why I wanted to let you know what the plans were. The builders will start first thing on Monday, and they'll keep disruption to a minimum." I stood up. As far as I was concerned the subject was closed. I waved my papers around with a flourish. "I have the plans here if anyone wishes to cast an eye over them."

Gwyn fixed me with a hostile glare, but I waved

her concerns away. "There's absolutely nothing to worry about," I trilled.

Famous last words.

The builders began work in *The Throne Room* at 8.30 a.m. Right from the off I knew something wasn't right.

It was nothing concrete. I couldn't put my finger on why I felt uneasy. The builders came in and measured and re-measured the walls, consulted plans, tutted, shook their heads, sucked their teeth and measured some more. There were only two of them, a bobble-hat-wearing older chap by the name of Neil, and a younger lad named Joe, his apprentice, who sported a full on-beard. Finally, after a great deal of to-ing and fro-ing and numerous cups of tea, they got down to business. Neil, as head honcho, chalked an outline on the wall, a ghostly sketch of where the door would be.

And it was at that stage that I felt a little unnerved. Until that moment, I had never experienced anything untoward in that particular bedroom. The inn was absolutely riddled with ghosts, and for the most part there had never been any issues. Yet, as the time came for the builders to cut through the wall, I experienced a pang of anxiety.

"This is well-weird," Joe was saying.

"Why?" I asked. He brandished the plans at me, and Neil snatched them out of his hands.

"I think what he's trying to say, Miss *Demon*, is that the measurements don't quite match up." He lay the plans on the wide window ledge and I went over to take a look. "See here." The older builder ran a stubby finger with a badly broken nail over the paper. "You've got your bathroom there, next door like, and the bedroom here. Notice anything?"

I scanned the plans but couldn't see anything odd.

"This is the outer wall." The hairy-knuckled, fat finger, floated along the corridor wall. I could see where the doors to the various rooms had been inked in. "Well, it stands to reason that the width of the two rooms, plus the partition wall equals that measurement there. Do you see?"

Yes, now I thought I knew what he was getting at. The area on either side of the wall would stay constant, only the length of the rooms would change. "But they don't?"

"Not even close, love. We've got that room there,

that measures three-point-two metres across, and this room that measures four-point-four metres and the wall along the corridor that measures nine-point-two-metres."

"But there's the actual wall measurement to take into account, right?"

"For sure. But your intervening wall ain't going to be over a metre thick, is it?"

I looked at the wall thoughtfully. "Bricked up fireplace?" I was thinking aloud. It was a rational idea but flawed given there was already an open fire-place in this bedroom on the opposite wall. Adjacent rooms shared fireplace space, and both fed up to one chimney.

"Nah," the builder said. I sensed he was rather enjoying himself.

"Cupboard then?" Now I was being hopeful.

"Could be. Although I think that would be unusual in a building of this age."

"What then? Secret room?"

The builder smirked. "I think it's a little too small to be a secret room, but we'll know when we open it up. Won't we?"

I ran my hand over the wall. Silvan would have known how to reveal what lay behind this space, but I didn't understand enough specific magick to do that. I looked around for Gwyn, but she was nowhere in sight.

"I guess so," I replied and reluctantly stepped away from the wall.

"We'll let you know what we find." The young builder smiled cheerily, and I understood he had dismissed me. I had to let them get on with it.

"Smashing." I took the hint and headed for my office.

I perched on the chair in front of my desk wondering what to start with first, knowing that within minutes the inn would reverberate to the sound of sledgehammers and drills. It would probably be loud, and it would certainly be disruptive. Perhaps I'd go in search of Finbarr and we could walk the perimeter fence together. Given that my cold seemed to have disappeared, I quite fancied a walk out in Speckled Wood.

I'd half made up my mind to do just that when the banging started. They were knocking through from the bedroom. I wondered what they would find? A long-neglected fireplace or a cavity in the wall?

But then the thumping stopped and even from my distance down the hall I distinctly heard the young builder say, "Maaaaaaaaaaaaate," in a disbelieving tone.

This was followed by a muffled consultation. I put my head in my hands and waited.

I didn't have to wait long. The sound of heavy boots clumping along the corridor were followed by a hasty tapping on the door. The young builder, ashen-faced, popped his head through the gap before I could invite him to come in. I looked up at him through splayed fingers.

"Erm, we think you should take a look at this?"

"What is it?" I asked but he'd already turned tail. I took a deep breath and followed him, hopeful that whatever they had found was some kind of Whittle Inn treasure, but knowing in my heart it probably wasn't.

As I entered *The Throne Room*, I could see that the builders had made quite a sizeable hole very quickly, like a large window. The elder builder was carefully removing wattle and daub from around the outside of the hole to make it bigger.

"What have you found?" I asked and he beckoned me over.

I carefully picked my way through the debris on

the floor and placed my hand against the wall for support so that I could lean forward. As I peered into the gap, looking down into the gloomy shadows, I noted the faint traces of some kind of magickal pulse. At some stage an enchantment had bound this space to secrecy. My elbow connected with the edge of the hole, sending plaster dust and old straw scattering into the dark vacuum below. The wall did not have any sort of thickness, it was little more than wood and straw and plaster.

The elder builder handed me a torch and I flicked it on...

... and gasped.

A corpse.

My brain reeled at what it thought it was seeing. Not a body as such but a skeleton. All the flesh had fortunately wasted away, leaving behind dry white bones. It had obviously been in situ for a long time. There were a number of items scattered around it.

Whomever it had been, male or female, had been wearing robes of a saffron orange colour, with a pointed hat in matching material. These marked it out as a witch or a wizard.

I strangled a moan in my throat and reared back in shock. Who the devil had boarded up a witch in these walls? And why?

Such an horrific end. What kind of a witch would sanction that ending for another?

What kind of a Daemonne? Because surely my ancestors must have authorised this. It couldn't have happened without their knowledge.

"We need to call the police." The builder's voice broke into my thoughts.

I had to agree. I turned to tell him I'd do that and noted Gwyn behind him. She looked in horror at the hole in the wall, and as I moved away she floated into my place. The builders couldn't see her. They didn't know she was there. I watched Gwyn put her hands to her throat and utter a blessing. Tears formed in her eyes.

"The police?" Joe asked again.

There was no covering this up. No tidying it away with magick. Nothing Wizard Shadowmender could do to help me here.

"I have one on speed dial," I said and reached for my mobile.

Chapter Five

It seemed strange having George back at the inn. He proceeded to take charge of the police operation with quiet and studious professionalism. I expected nothing less of him, but once or twice he caught my eye and something complicated and unresolved passed between us.

He had arrived fairly quickly, along with his young sidekick Danny, whom I vaguely recognised. Once he'd ascertained that I hadn't gone crazy, and there really was a skeleton in my walls, he had gotten straight onto the phone and requested the attendance of a forensic team. Before I knew what was happening, I had people clad in white plastic suits and slippers cordoning off the corridor and *The Throne Room*. Cameras flashed constantly for some time, and then several people began sweeping the bare wood floor and the walls with what looked like a giant laser wand.

I had positioned myself in the corridor where I could see what was going on. George stepped back to have a word, with his pen and notebook at the ready.

"When did you get back?" he asked, and I wondered whether it was for his records or because he was hurt that I hadn't been in touch.

I licked my lips, my mouth dry. I couldn't tell whether this was as a result of the shock of finding the skeleton, or from seeing George up close in this way. It had been a while. "Last weekend." It sounded deliberately vague. I didn't want to hurt him.

"Oh." He still managed to sound disappointed. "I haven't heard from you."

"I've had quite a bit going on and I haven't been well."

"Witch flu, I heard?" I saw a smile play out at the edge of his lips. He'd been talking to Charity. Were those two in cahoots?

I decided to change the subject, indicating the activity in the bedroom in front of us. "Now this."

George nodded and quickly scanned what he had written down. "You had no idea there was anything behind this wall?"

Was he crazy? "Certainly not. I'd hardly have called the builders in to knock it through if I'd..."

George held his hand up in a peace gesture. "I'm not suggesting you had anything to do with putting the body there. Quite clearly it's been there a very long time. I'm just asking whether you knew it was there."

I folded my arms in defiance. "Well no then. I didn't."

"Okay." George wrote that down. "And for my records, Whittle Inn has been in your family for how long?"

"Since forever." He knew that, but he gave me a look nonetheless. "Erm ... the written records date back to the 1400s," I expanded.

George nodded, and regarded me quizzically. "And..." he nodded at Gwyn, pacing among the forensic team as they carried out their investigation. George could see the ghosts, of course. I'd helped him to do that when we'd first started seeing each other, but the rest of his team could not. "Have there been any rumours... in the family... handed down, say... of anything untoward that happened in the past? Anything that needed covering up?"

The truth was of course that Whittle Inn and the Daemonne family were inextricably and eternally linked. We seemed to thrive on secrets and hidden truths. It sometimes appeared as though I learned something new about my family history every day.

I watched Gwyn darting about in agitation and I instinctively understood that she knew what had happened here. Or knew *something* about it at least. Perhaps she wasn't to blame, but she did hold the key.

"No," I replied honestly. "I've never heard anything regarding a corpse in the walls of the inn, or even of an unexplained death or a missing person."

I shook my head, tears not far away. A wave of sadness began to overwhelm me.

"It's okay, Alf," George said gently. "You understand I have to ask these questions."

"Of course!" I said and gritted my teeth, blinking my eyes rapidly before taking a deep breath. "There is one thing..."

"Yes?"

"The body... what's left of it... is wearing robes." I glanced around to make sure Danny couldn't hear us and lowered my voice to a whisper. "That probably means they were a witch or a wizard."

"Or dressing up," George suggested.

I tutted and pulled a face at him.

"I have to cover all eventualities," George pointed out.

I growled at him. "Well maybe, but in *this* inn? With *my* family? You reckon?"

"No, you're probably right." He looked back into the room where one of the forensic team was removing a number of items from around the skeleton and slipping them into plastic evidence bags.

"How long do you think it has been there?" I asked.

"We don't know yet. I'll have to let the pathologist determine that."

"And cause of death?"

"Yes. Nothing obvious at the moment. But when all you're left with are the bones, it can be incredibly difficult to work that out."

I placed my hand on George's arm. "Would you be able to let me know when you do find out? Only... if I know *when* the body was left there, that might help us work out *who* left it."

George patted my hand. "I'll tell you what I can, when I can. That's the best I can do."

"Good enough," I said, and wished I could fold myself into his arms for a reassuring hug. Maybe he felt the same way because his hand hesitated, remaining on mine. But those days were over for now and I wasn't sure they would ever return, so I pulled away and went in search of a tissue.

Either my cold was coming back, or I was weepy. One of the two.

His forensic team were thorough. They carefully removed the remainder of the wall so they could gain access to the space beyond. At some stage *The Throne Room* had been bigger than it now was, and one of my ancestors had added the partition to house their terrible secret.

The pieces of the wall were taken away for further examination, and I watched as a plastic clad woman examined the remaining surfaces with painstaking detail, armed with a torch, a camera and a pair of tweezers.

With the wall down, the exposed space was the height and the length of the room, and just over a metre wide. More photos were taken of the skeleton in situ, and then the body was recovered, and carefully placed inside a body bag for removal to the mortuary.

We all stood in respectful silence as two funeral

directors bore the body away on behalf of the coroner. I dashed at another tear as I watched them gently manoeuvre the stretcher down the stairs.

Then more photos were taken of the objects that had been revealed by the removal of the skeleton in its voluminous robes. I spotted a book—black leather and covered in dust. One of the forensic scientists picked it up and something fell from among the pages, floating down onto the grimy floor. Some kind of black and white photo by the look of it. I couldn't get close enough to see any detail.

I watched Gwyn shoot through the air to stand alongside the scientist as she reached down to pick up the photograph and study it. For once I envied my great-grandmother's invisibility. I found myself burning with curiosity to examine both the book and the photo. No doubt they would yield interesting clues.

Finally, just after seven that evening, the corridor was released back to me, although George instructed me to keep the bedroom locked up until he and his team had finished with it. "For at least the next few days," he suggested. "But maybe longer."

I nodded, feeling glum. So much for my plans for the bathrooms then.

I rang the builders, who had been sent home

earlier in the day, to put them off for the time being. We would resume the renovations as soon as humanly possible.

Charity and the rest of my staff continued to service our guests, trying to act normally, but the mood over my wonky inn remained subdued all night, each of us no doubt thinking of the unknown victim in this sad situation, imagining how he or she had ended up there.

I spent a long time in my office that evening, nursing a brandy and staring blankly at the pages of a novel I'd started reading while on holiday. At some stage I became aware that Gwyn was restless too. She haunted the corridor outside my room, disappearing every so often into *The Throne Room,* but when I tried to question her about what she knew and why she was so upset, she apparated away from me, only to return five minutes later and repeat the process.

Over and over.

Later I lay in bed, the window open, listening to Mr Hoo hunting in the distance, puzzling over the day's events.

I couldn't help but feel responsible in some way and I wanted to know what had happened so that the inn, or I at least, could make reparations. Of course, given the state of the body and the advanced decomposition, there was every possibility that it had been holed up and hidden away for a long time, maybe decades before I'd been born.

I didn't get much sleep that night.

CHAPTER SIX

We muddled on, something we were adept at doing at Whittle Inn. *The Throne Room* remained closed up, with police officers intermittently returning and conducting more tests and further investigation, but the corridor and *Neverwhere* were released back to me. The builders came back and continued what they'd started. There were additional expenses involved. Given the amount of fingerprint dust everywhere, and as a direct result of both the police investigation and the building works, before I knew it the whole floor, with the exception of my own suite of rooms, needed to be painted and decorated.

Both the dust and the furore settled, but the memory of the anonymous skeleton formed a hard chunk of ice in my stomach. I needed to do something, anything, even if this 'something' only amounted to finding a name.

Ten days after the discovery George rang me to ask whether I'd like to meet him for a drink. Ostensibly he suggested we would discuss his initial findings and he'd run a few more questions past me, things that might help him pursue a few leads, but secretly I think we both wanted to take some time to test out our feelings about our muted relationship.

We'd pressed pause. Was it time to hit play?

It seemed important to meet on neutral ground, and rather than show my face at *The Hay Loft*, Whittle Inn's rival in Whittlecombe, I drove to *The Blue Bell Inn* in Durscombe and found my way to the snug at the rear of the inn. Only a few months had elapsed since George and I had listened to the Devonshire Fellows for the very first time in the same spot, but now the entire band of Fellows resided at Whittle Inn.

George had obviously had the same idea, because he had taken a place at exactly the same table. *The Blue Bell* was busy, serving meals to hungry tourists, so we were lucky to have a table at all. He stood as I arrived and gave me a hug. It felt natural and I relaxed into it momentarily.

"You've forgiven me for turning you into a toad,

then?" I asked when we'd both settled and had drinks in front of us.

He gave me a look that was hard to read. "You know after everything that happened to me, I'm not even sure that inhabiting the body of a toad was that much of a big deal. There wasn't a lot to worry about. Eat, sleep, swim, repeat."

I grinned. "Vance looked after you."

"Yes, he did." George shook his head in wonder. "What a creature he is."

I nodded. The Keeper of the Marsh was hundreds of years old and a real character. I hadn't been to see him since I'd arrived back from my holiday, but I ought to. I knew he'd appreciate a chat.

"Is Jed still out there with him?" George asked, and I nodded.

"I think that's safest." Jed would have to be turned over to The Circle of Querkus if I reinstated him to human form and that seemed unnecessary. He'd saved my life after all. "Wizard Shadowmender knows where to find him if he really wants him."

"Pretty surreal." George drank deeply from his pint, and then regarded me over the top of his glass. "You know, in spite of everything that's happened, I'm not sorry that I met you."

"I'm glad." I held a nervous giggle in check. It

sounded like something someone would say if they never wanted to see you again.

George hesitated. I waited. Then there was a roar of laughter from the bar area behind us and the moment was lost. Instead he pulled his notebook, pen, and a plastic evidence bag from his jacket pocket.

"I wanted to fill you in on where we are with the skeleton we found at the inn." He'd adopted his professional and formal tone and there was a part of me that ached to hear it. I swallowed the pain and slumped back in my chair, waiting to hear what he had to say.

"First of all, we are able to categorically state the skeleton is a male. His age... that's a whole different ballgame."

George flicked through his notepad and read his notes. "To be honest the post-mortem is inconclusive. The age of the bones is indeterminate, which the pathologist finds bizarre. She's running more tests. Initial test data suggests anything from thirty years to three hundred years, so we're wide off the mark somewhere."

"That won't help me narrow down when he stayed at the inn then?" *Strange.* "What about his age when he died?"

"Again, results are inconclusive. There are signs of aging in terms of fusion of certain bones, but also characteristics of a young man. We just don't know."

"Oh," I said. "What else have you found out about him?"

"No obvious sign of trauma. No damage to the bones."

I wasn't sure this could be construed as good news. If he hadn't been murdered before he was interred behind the wall, it didn't bear thinking about how long he'd been boarded up there awaiting rescue.

George tapped the plastic bag. "If you're up to it, I have a couple of things to show you." He unzipped the plastic bag and drew out the black leather book I'd seen the forensic scientist holding, along with several scene of crime photos.

Casting a quick look around to make sure no-one was watching us, he placed the photos in front of me. There was one of the skeleton as it had been found, wearing his robes and hat. Another showed the robes laid out on a white surface, clearly displaying the pattern and edging. "Do you recognise these robes?"

"Only in as much as I saw them on the day our friend was discovered," I replied, feeling sad for our anonymous victim. “He needs a name. It’s horrible that he’s so anonymous.”

“We just call them The Deceased.”

I looked pleadingly at George. “That’s just awful? Can we at least give him a temporary name?”

George frowned but I could see he would humour me. “What would your suggestion be?”

I lifted the photo and studied the image. “He needs a name that is timeless. Something old that could also be new. How about Luke?”

“Luke it is then. But just between us, alright?” George gave me a warning look and I nodded.

“Of course.”

“Going back to these robes that... Luke... is wearing. Do you think they’re the genuine article?”

“As in something a witch or wizard would wear?”

“Yes.”

“I do.” I pointed at the hemline, the colours would once have been vibrant: orange, several shades of blue and deep purple, shot through with a gold silk. “This is exquisite. I’m willing to bet these cost a bit and were made by the best tailors in the business.”

“So not fancy dress?”

I shuddered to think that some innocent mortal

had found their way into the inn wearing fancy dress and been finished off by one of my forebears. "I really don't think so, George."

"Fair enough." George shuffled those photos together and offered me the book to have a look at. I'd imagined from a distance that it had to be an old classic and I wasn't wrong. A first edition of Bram Stoker's *Dracula*, the gilt lettering faded. I opened the cover to find a name in neat cursive writing, Alfhild Gwynfyre.

"Grandmama?" I ran my fingertips gently over the two words there. Gwynfyre. This had been her book before she'd married my great-grandfather.

"I don't understand," I choked the words out. "I can't believe my great-grandmother would do this."

George leaned forward and placed his hand on my knee, his voice soft. "There's no need to upset yourself, Alf. No-one is insinuating anything about Gwyn, and even if she was implicated somehow, to everyone except you she's been gone a long, long time."

"You don't understand, George. Everyone else is not me. It's not Charity. It's not *you* even." I'd raised my voice and people were looking around at us. I reined myself in and spoke more quietly. "We know her. She's as real to us as the people at the next table."

George nodded. "There is that."

"I'll try and talk to her about it, but she's been avoiding me ever since Luke was found. You know what she's like for disappearing on me."

"Right. Yes. See what you can find out. There may be something she knows that would help us identify who this is. That's probably the most important thing given that we're looking—more than likely—at a historic death."

"I will try," I repeated, not holding out much hope. I reached for my glass. I'd only ordered an orange juice spritzer given that I was driving. My hand shook slightly, and I wished I'd had a brandy instead.

"There was this as well." George held out another photograph. "This was tucked inside the book."

He handed over a marvellous sepia toned photograph on heavy card. Three men and a woman were standing outside the inn. My breath caught in my throat. I was definitely looking at an image of a young Gwyn. We looked similar, although I couldn't tell her hair colouring from the photograph. She wasn't smiling, none of them were, but she didn't look unhappy.

"That's Gwyn," I confirmed.

"And the men?"

"Well," I pursed my lips and regarded each one in turn. "I'm going to hazard a guess that one of them is my great-grandfather, James Daemonne. I don't think I've ever seen a picture of him before. I don't recognise any of them." I flipped the photo over. *July 1920. GG, WW, AGD, JD.* "AGD and JD? That would confirm two of these people as my great grandparents, I suppose."

"But who are GG and WW?"

I shrugged. "I have no idea."

WW though? That was a coincidence.

I sat at my desk with the closed briefcase in front of me, fiddling with the little tag.

The property of W Wylie.

WW.

But we couldn't be talking about the W Wylie that had stayed at Whittle Inn back in March.

Could we?

"You're burning the midnight oil, Miss Alf."

Startled, I glanced up. Florence hovered in the doorway, her ever-present feather duster swinging through the air in front of her.

"I am rather." I yawned and stretched. "It's a bit late to be up dusting, Florence."

My housekeeper grinned, slightly sheepishly. "I know. I'm trying to catch up."

I nodded but didn't say anything. I'd figured Florence would eventually grow tired of all the Witchflix programmes and return to her *duties*. If she wanted to. If she didn't, then who was I to judge? Florence had lived a short mortal life, there was no point in being miserable for all eternity in her afterlife.

I indicated the briefcase in front of me. "Do you remember this?"

Florence floated in, close enough I could have touched her, had she been a physical entity. "The briefcase?"

"Cast your mind back to when I stayed down at the Psychic Fayre and left you Charity and Gwyn to run the inn. Do you remember?"

"Oh, I do!" Florence exclaimed excitedly. "You had me spy on a gentleman for you."

Hooray! Someone remembered. I wasn't going crazy.

"Tell me what you remember," I said.

"We thought he seemed a little strange and out of place. He told us he wanted to stay at *The Hay Loft*, but of course they were full, so he came to us instead. He didn't appear to be our normal kind of guest."

"Do you remember his name?"

Florence paused while she racked her brains. "Mr Wylie."

Bingo.

"What did he look like?" I asked, curious because I had never met him and yet now his name kept turning up.

Florence swished her duster around on my desk through force of habit, even though she knew I hated her tidying the office. "He wasn't very tall. Not like Mr George or Mr Silvan. Perhaps he was around Charity's height."

"Okay." I held my hand up to stop the onslaught of the feather duster.

"Sorry." Florence regained control of the dastardly implement. "He was dark-haired like Mr Silvan, but very neat. Not like Mr Silvan." Silvan was a free spirit and his tousle of hair very much reflected that. "His hair was short, and he had a tidy moustache." She mimed a moustache sitting on a top lip. "He always dressed very well, in a smart suit."

"Like Ross Baines?" I asked.

"Oooh the lovely Ross Baines," Florence smiled. I knew she had taken quite a shine to Ross. Sadly, he'd left us to go and work for Penelope Quigwell and I'd heard through the grapevine that he was getting on very well in her team of technical wizards —the first ghost she'd ever employed. "Perhaps not as smart as Ross."

I took that with a pinch of salt. "And you recall that I asked you to look in his briefcase?" I asked. "Is this the same briefcase?" I pointed to the case.

Florence looked doubtful, probably wondering why that briefcase would have turned up on my desk. "I'm not sure I'd remember, Miss Alf," she said, her face crestfallen.

"No." I felt disappointed myself. But why would one briefcase be any different to another?

"Except..." Florence suddenly bent at the waist, her head disappearing into the briefcase. I saw her look sideways, left then right, and then she stood upright once more. "I am certain this is the same one," she announced looking pleased with herself.

"How can you be so sure?" I popped the clasps and eased the lid up. Without a magickal command, the briefcase remained empty. Nothing to see at all. No distinguishing marks as far as I could tell.

"In the little cloth pocket there." Florence pointed. "Purple and white striped paperclips."

I dug my hand into the pocket, reaching deep with my fingers. And yes, there were several paperclips inside. I drew them out. Purple and white.

"Well done, Florence. I'm impressed as always with your amateur sleuthing skills."

Florence curtsied in delight and beamed at me.

"This is the same briefcase then?" she enquired.

"It would certainly seem so."

I just couldn't comprehend why it kept turning up.

Like a bad penny.

CHAPTER SEVEN

Given the way the Psychic Fayre had ended—with an arson attack on local man Rob Parker's Porky Perfection sausage van, and lots of bad feeling towards some of the supposed fortune tellers on site—I was surprised to discover that the villagers had decided that the annual Apple Pie Fair would go ahead as normal over the late Bank Holiday weekend.

On a much smaller scale than the Psychic Fayre, and occupying just one field, the Apple Pie Fair had a long history in the village; dating back to Tudor times and the earliest settlements in the area. People came together every year in celebration of the humble apple. This being the west country, there was plenty of locally brewed cider, both fizzy and cloudy—pretty potent in some cases—as well as pies and puddings and preserves, all of which had been made using locally grown apples.

In many ways this fair marked the cusp between late summer and early Autumn. Children could try their hand at bobbing for apples in large plastic troughs, or snap apples which involved trying to catch apples hung on strings from the branches of a tree with your mouth. There was an apple shy where young men could vent their frustrations by throwing small apples at piles of windfalls artfully arranged on a dais. Or an 'apple press' which required ladies to take off their socks and shoes and enter a large wooden press, where they walked round and round and crushed the apples underfoot.

I admit to being intrigued by this. Local folklore suggested that in the old days only the younger village women and older girls had performed this task, and it had been some sort of rite of passage. A way to catch the eye of some hunky agricultural worker perhaps.

When the proprietor of the press caught me looking, he waved me over to give it a go, but I decided for the sake of my own sanity to give it a wide berth. I wasn't in the mood to catch the eye of any man just at the moment, thank you. Relationships, I'd decided, were the cause of too much angst.

So, like the old spinster I rapidly appeared to be turning into—and not caring one jot anyway—I circled the field in search of Millicent.

And there she was, proudly displaying her own large number of appley-type potions alongside her own edibles. As she appeared to be busy, I joined her at her stall to help out. Millicent was well respected in the community, someone whom many people liked to turn to for minor coughs and colds and such like, so I wasn't surprised at how popular her wares were. I fiddled with her colourful display, beautifully packaged with handwritten labels, and decorated with twists of home-dyed rattan string and tiny posies of late summer flowers. I inspected with great interest the *Potion for the Easement of Muscle Aches*, the *Potion for the Eradication of Verrucae and Corns*, the *Wish-a-Mole-Away Body Wash*, not to mention the *Banish your Blues Bubble Bath* and the *Mute Miserable Memories Mouth Tonic*.

"No blackberry cordial?" I asked. "It worked a treat for me."

Millicent regarded me from under a wide-brimmed purple sunhat carelessly strewn with clashing orange felt star shapes. "I've run out of plague cadaver samples."

I grimaced. "You told me you were kidding about that!"

"You're so gullible, Alfhild." Millicent straightened the table cloth and avoided looking at me, so I couldn't tell whether she meant I'd been gullible then, or I was being gullible now. I decided I didn't want to find out.

"Shall I go and buy us a cup of tea?" I asked instead.

Millicent laughed. "No! You only just arrived here, and we haven't made enough money yet. Why don't you concentrate on selling the merchandise?"

For the next hour I did as she suggested. I don't have a problem with being passionate about food, and many a time I'd enjoyed Millicent's hospitality, so selling the cakes and preserves came easily to me. Millicent had baked her usual array of Victoria sponges, as well as fairy cakes, brownies and blondies, and flapjacks. She had also offered to sell cakes and bread for the ladies in her WI group, so our tables groaned under the combined weight of some seriously impressive baked items. I let Millicent attend to those who needed something a little more potent–and was amazed at just how popular her medicinals and potions proved to be.

When trade slowed down briefly, I excused

myself. I partly wanted to take the opportunity to explore the fair a little more, and possibly spend some money on the raffle or the hook-a-duck. I also desperately needed to quench my thirst so intended to grab that cup of tea after all.

Millicent waved me away in amusement and I skirted around the apple press once more, giggling at the girls with their summer dresses tucked into their knickers and squealing at the cold slimy squishiness of the apple pulp between their toes.

I waited patiently to buy some tickets at the raffle table. There were the usual boxes of chocolates and bottles of wine, a couple of soft toys and some unwanted Christmas gift sets. Nothing I particularly desired, but all proceeds were split between local charities, so I felt it important to support them. Whittle Inn had sent down a couple of bottles of spirits and one of Florence's special cakes, a magnificent raspberry and white chocolate gateaux. Now I wouldn't have minded winning that back, but I guess that just wouldn't have been British.

In the centre of the field, a square had been roped off and a group of children were engaging in a tug-of-war, marshalled I was pleased to note, by Stan from Whittle Stores. He'd finally recovered from his poisoning in the toxic waters of Whittle Folly, and although he had lost a great deal of weight, his wife Rhona assured me he was going to be fine in the long term.

On the opposite side of the field to Millicent, I had another pleasant surprise when I found a van with fancy green and gold livery. It seemed Parker's Porky Perfection, a sausage catering wagon, was back in business. I skipped over and beamed at him when it was my time to be served but of course, he really only knew my Fabulous Fenella guise. Even though as Alf I was his landlady, we hadn't really gotten to know each other with me as myself.

I ordered two teas and carried them over to a small side table where all the sachets of sauces and little paper packets of salt and pepper and sugar were kept, so that I could steep the tea and add a sugar to each. It was at that stage that I became aware of someone watching me.

I glanced up and peered into the throng of people in front of me. Some were engaged with the tombola, others were heading for the display ring. There were some Brownie Guides manning a book-stall. It wasn't immediately obvious to me who had been looking my way.

My witch twitch was on high alert though. Feeling a little anxious, memories of The Mori fresh in my mind, I reached out with my senses, seeking the party interested in me. At first, I could feel nothing and almost dropped my search. Humans have an innate ability—almost a sixth sense which developed in prehistoric times to help them survive—to sense a full face, human or animal, when it is turned upon them. Witches are able to utilise that sense further.

I was about to dismiss my exploration when I scuffed the edges of someone else's magickal persona. Too close to my position to be Millicent, I doubled my efforts to scan the crowds.

Then I spotted him.

A man of average height, tidy haircut and a neat moustache. Wearing a suit. At a village fete? Who wears a suit in a country field? That's what gave it away.

He met my eyes with a frank and open stare, as though he had nothing to hide and I had nothing to fear. Nevertheless, my hand found its way into my pocket and curled around my wand. The lessons I'd learned with Silvan would always stand me in good stead. Controlling the adrenaline that might once have threatened to overwhelm me, I softened my knees and breathed easily.

He glanced behind himself then took a few steps

back, holding his hands up in a peace gesture. I released the hold on my wand, picked up my teas and followed him. I caught up with him just before the display area. A troupe of young children, wearing sparkly shorts and t-shirts, were about to begin a dance display. They stood in lines, a few giggling nervously, others waving at parents and siblings in the crowd.

He waited for me, on the periphery of the crowd, making an effort to blend in, but failing. Wearing that suit meant people were looking twice at him, when they would otherwise have barely noticed him. Close up, I observed his clothing was strangely old fashioned, the jacket a longer length than men chose to wear today, and the shirt collar stiff and oddly formal.

"Mr W Wylie, I presume?" I asked as I reached him. I was guessing, but the description that Florence had given me tallied well.

He gave a quick nod of his head, his eyes scanning the crowd. It struck me then how anxious he was. He didn't appear to be any sort of threat to me, but it seemed clear that he considered I—or someone else around us—might be a threat to him.

"I have your briefcase," I told him. He raised a finger to his lips, and I fell silent. We turned to watch the children. There appeared to be a problem with piping music over the tannoy and so the display had been held up. Some of the kids were becoming restless. One little lad pulled his neighbour's pig-tails and I worried she would start to cry.

We stood shoulder to shoulder, he was slightly shorter than me, and he leaned over a little to speak low in my ear without looking at me. "I need your help."

"Alright," I replied. I would always try and help anyone in need if I could. "How can I do that?"

"I left something at your inn."

Was that all? "Well, by all means come and collect it. We have a substantial amount of lost property in storage. We—"

"It was hidden."

"When you stayed before?" I was confused. "Seriously... Why not just come to the inn?"

"I've tried to find it and failed. I need to know if you have found it or whether it's been removed?"

I looked sideways at him. The man was making no sense. He hadn't been back to the inn since the Psychic Fayre. Not as far as I knew anyway. Although the missing reservation suggested someone had been tampering with my records.

"What is it you've lost?" Perhaps if I knew that I could help him.

He tugged at his moustache in agitation. "I'm sorry. I really can't say."

I turned to him and he ducked away as though I would strike him. I held my hands palm-up in concern, trying to quell his nerves. "Mr Wylie—"

He took a step back, his eyes wide. "You don't understand. It's dangerous for me to be out in the open like this." His eyes darted around the crowd. I followed his anxious gaze wondering who or what he was looking for.

"Mr Wylie, let me help."

He looked at me properly for the first time. We locked gazes. His eyes were a deep dark blue, the colour of a night sky. The sparkles I could see there reminded me of the stars. Entrancing.

"How do I know I can trust you?" he whispered. "Trusting people doesn't always end well."

I recognised that feeling. "I won't let you down," I tried to promise him. "If you're on the level with me."

He edged closer and I turned to face him so that we were almost chest to chest, his lips level with my chin. "Did you find my friend?"

A loud bang from behind me startled us both. I

dropped my teas and reached for my wand, swinging about. A couple of metres from me a child opened her mouth and began to scream. A forlorn string draped from her hand, flaccid rubber lying in the grass beneath her feet. Her balloon had popped.

I laughed shakily. "It's alright." I swivelled back to Mr Wylie to reassure him, but he'd disappeared. I turned around and about, slowly, trying to see which way he'd gone, peering into the groups of people milling around the fete with their ice creams and tombola prizes. I used my witch senses, attempting to sense the trail he'd taken but I could find no trace.

He'd dissipated into the ether.

I arrived back at the inn a few hours later laden down with some of the produce Millicent hadn't been able to sell, a sad looking pastel pink soft toy I'd won in the raffle, and a bottle of freshly pressed cider vinegar for Monsieur Emietter to try out at some stage. My feet were killing me after all the standing up and walking around, but I needed to help out with dinner service before I found some time to relax.

Eventually, clutching my soft toy—I hadn't had a

teddy bear for years—I climbed the stairs to my bedroom and popped him on my bed. Mr Hoo, from his place on the bedstead, eyed the usurper with great distrust.

"I'm sure you'll become great friends," I told the owl, scratching his head. He produced his familiar twitting sound and seemed content enough. "I'm going to call her Blossom. Like apple blossom. That's a nice name, isn't it?"

"Hooooo."

I smiled. "My feet are like plates of meat." I threw myself on to my bed and pulled off my shoes and stockings. "I could do with a foot massage. I don't think either of you can help me with that." I glanced out of the window, thinking about George. Then Jed. My stomach squeezed with dismay as I considered what I'd had and lost.

"Some things just aren't meant to be," I told myself softly. "Perhaps they aren't real. Were never real. Perhaps they were too real." I sighed. "What do I know? I know nothing about love."

Sudden tears surprised me. I dashed them away in annoyance, determined not to give in to such maudlin feelings.

"I'm going to run a bath," I announced to Mr Hoo and Blossom, and slipped into my en-suite to turn the taps on. I picked up a jar of bath milk, a freesia and basil concoction that Millicent had gifted me, and poured it into the water, watching as the milk bloomed into clouds that rolled and broiled in the water forming shapes and images. Naturally I allowed what I saw there to suggest meaning... What sort of witch would I be if I didn't take every opportunity to divine my world?

I frowned to see Mr Wylie there among the billowing clouds, and as I lifted my head to think about the encounter I'd had with him at the Apple Pie Fair earlier in the day, I knew without a shadow of a doubt that he was somewhere with me now at Whittle Inn.

I turned the taps off and dried my hands, then padded out into the corridor that ran the length of the first floor in my bare feet, looking up and down it. No ghosts. Nobody around at all. I could hear music coming from downstairs, gentle Elizabethan music. Luppitt Smeatharpe, alone, playing to our guests in the bar.

From above me came the sounds of people walking around in their rooms, the creak and groan of old timbers and wooden floors. But on this floor only silence. I walked slowly along the corridor. Beside my rooms—bedroom, bathroom and office with its little kitchenette that I had never had occasion to use—there were eight guest rooms on this floor. Two small ones and six that I considered 'state rooms' because they were larger. Three of them had their own turret. One of these was the unfortunate *Throne Room*. For now, it was still closed up and awaiting some love and attention. I made a mental note to contact George again and ask whether the police could release it back to me.

I paused outside the door, resting the palm of my hand on the cool painted surface. I reached out, feeling the energy in the room beyond, sensed the slight movement within, the minute disruption of the air on the other side of the wood. Mr Wylie was inside.

I gently turned the handle and walked in. The lighting in the room was subdued but I could clearly make out Mr Wylie, standing in front of the large hole in the wall, peering inside. He turned without surprise. He'd expected me to join him.

"I didn't imagine I'd find you here tonight." I kept my voice low. "You know I mean you no harm. I meant what I said at the Fair. I'd like to help you if I can."

I stepped closer to him and realised in horror that he was crying. Tears sparkled brightly as they ran from his eyes, damp trails shimmered on his cheeks.

"Mr Wylie? Are you alright?" I asked, panicking that he'd been hurt in some way.

He pointed at the gap in the wall, at the place where we'd found the skeleton. "Is that where my friend was? What happened to him? Did you find—?"

"Alf?"

Charity was in the corridor, looking for me. Like a fool I'd left the door open behind me. I turned to shut the door. As I did so, a flash of blue light brightened the room, and from the corner of my eye I noticed Mr Wylie suddenly spinning rapidly. In the time it took me to turn back to look at him properly, he'd disappeared.

"Mr Wylie?" I called. "Mr Wylie? I'm sorry. Come back." But I was talking to empty air.

Charity heard me calling and popped her head around the open door, looking at me curiously, evidently wondering what I was doing all alone in this room.

"Sorry, Alf," she said. "Hope I'm not interrupting." She waited and I could tell she wanted to find out what I was up to. "Are you looking for someone?"

I shook my head. "What's up?" Frustration at the

turn of events bubbled inside me. What had Mr Wylie been trying to ask? What had he lost? Who was his friend?"

Charity pouted. Admittedly, it was unlike me to keep her out of the loop. "I can't find the key to the cellar. Do you have a spare?"

I nodded. "On my desk." I led her back to the office and rummaged underneath a large pile of paperclips, rubber bands, memos, business cards and post-it notes until I found it. Hard to lose given that it was eight inches of black iron. "Where's the other one got to?"

"Maybe Florence has it," Charity said. "I can't find her."

No doubt Florence was holed up somewhere watching Witchflix. "I'll find her," I said and nodded as Charity left.

I made a half-hearted attempt to straighten my desk again, and while doing so uncovered the copies of the photos that George had given me.

I picked up the one of Gwyn with the man I assumed had been her husband and the two strangers. I laughed, startled. Now that I'd met him in the flesh so to speak, I could see that the man to the immediate right of her was indeed Mr W Wylie.

But how could that be? The photo had been

taken a century ago. The Mr Wylie I'd met hadn't aged a bit, but he patently wasn't a ghost either.

It made no sense to me.

I moved through into my bedroom to extract my orb from its box in the wardrobe, my rapidly cooling bath all but forgotten.

I had a few calls to make.

CHAPTER EIGHT

I relaxed back into the soft leather chair clutching the pretty cup and saucer Mr Kephisto had offered me along with a handful of custard creams.

"And you say you haven't seen him again?" The elderly wizard was asking me. We were sitting in his attic room, surrounded by tomes and tomes of his research. Leather-backed books with gold lettering. Cardboard folders containing hundreds of pages of handwritten notes. Journals, diaries, account books, scrapbooks, boxes of photos or lithographs, original art and prints. Mr Kephisto was a one-wizard encyclopaedia of everything to do with the witching and wizarding world. As Wizard Shadowmender had told me when I'd contacted him through the orb the previous evening, if Mr Kephisto couldn't help me, then no-one could.

I shook my head, feeling solemn and oddly

guilty. "No. It's been two days and there's been no further contact from him." I dunked one of my biscuits. "I feel bad. He claimed that the bones we found in the room belonged to his friend, but he didn't give me any details." I munched thoughtfully. "It's an awful thing to find out one of your friends has been killed. And in that way? I feel desperately sorry for him."

Mr Kephisto reached over to take the photos I'd placed on the table between us. "You can't blame yourself, Alf. You had nothing to do with the death of the man." He lapsed into silence for a few moments as he studied the photos. "Your grandmother was a fine-looking woman."

"She still is," I said, swallowing a mouthful of deliciously flavoured vanilla crumbs.

"We always used to say James Daemonne had fallen on his feet when your great-grandmother agreed to marry him. He was a bit of a rogue was James."

In the process of lifting the cup to my mouth I paused in stunned silence and gazed at Mr Kephisto. What was he saying?

"I... You... What?"

"Just that she could have had her pick of any witch or wizard in the country, but she chose to leave

London and come to Devon to be with James at Whittle Inn." He smiled, lost in his memories. "Mind you, they threw a great wedding party. The pair of them were immense fun."

"You can't possibly have been there. That was... like... a hundred-and-something years ago."

"One hundred and two if I remember correctly."

I replaced my cup onto the saucer with a clatter and my tea sloshed over the edge. "I don't understand. I mean... I know you're old... but you can't be that old."

He'd alluded to his age before, but I'd never really taken any notice.

"Trust me. I'm a lot older than you think." He smiled. "I belong to a magickal order of guardians and it is our purpose to live long lives. Extremely long lives. But this isn't about me." He tapped the photo. "This is about these people. I knew your great-grandparents when they were alive. I'm delighted to still know your great-grandmother now. But I didn't know these two men." He gazed at the photo again, as though imprinting the image on his brain. "Or rather, I don't know them."

I don't know them? Continuous tense?

I struggled for a second. "You're suggesting that —like you—they're still alive?"

"Presumably this man," he indicated the chap on the far right of the photo, "is not. This may well be the friend that Mr Wylie alluded to."

We were grasping at straws.

"Is Mr Wylie a member of your order of guardians?" I asked.

"No." Mr Kephisto paused, gazing at me though the round lenses of his spectacles. I watched the cogs of his mind turn. He returned the photo to me and I studied it as he stood and went to his bookshelves, running his fingers gently along the spines, row after row, until eventually a slim dark-blue volume pushed itself out, away from the wall, the gilt lettering on the spine glowing. He plucked the book from his place and returned to his seat, the hard-board cover falling open, and the pages flipping quickly over—all of their own accord—as he scanned the contents.

At last he peered back up at me. "I'm going to hazard a guess that your Mr Wylie is a member of the Cosmic Order of Chronometric Wizards."

Cosmic Order?

I pursed my lips, a million questions forming there, but I was unsure which one to ask first. Eventually I settled for, "I've never heard of them."

"No reason why you should have," Mr Kephisto

replied cheerfully. "I'm certain they prefer it if no-one knows who they are."

"But they live a long time? Is that what you're saying?"

"Not at all." Mr Kephisto consulted the book in front of him again. "Far from it. They live a normal span—usually between sixty and a hundred years."

Hadn't we already established that the photo had been taken an extremely long time ago? This was making no sense. "But..."

Mr Kephisto grinned at me, a mischievous smile that brought a sparkle to his eye and caused his little round cheeks to flush adorably. "Chronometric Wizard is the clue here, Alf."

Chronometric. *Chronos*? Something to do with time? Coupled with the word cosmic, the realization came like a bolt out of the blue. "Time travel? Mr Wylie is a time-travelling wizard?" I couldn't quite believe that.

"That's my theory." Mr Kephisto nodded in satisfaction.

I leaned forwards, depositing my cup and saucer on the table, splashing more tea in the process. "What else does your book say about them?"

"There's not a great deal of information here. It was written by an investigative journalist on *The*

Celestine Times about thirty years ago. He drew on a number of sources for his information but reading between the lines, not much is evidence based or backed-up with detailed sources."

"That's disappointing."

"They're a small order of perhaps a hundred or so men and women, handpicked from graduates of The University of Somerset's Faculty of Witchery and Magick. They travel backwards and forwards in time to... ah... let's say create or repair certain situations."

"Create or repair? Meaning what exactly? They change time."

"You could say that, I suppose."

"Isn't that a bit dangerous? I mean you change one small thing and it has a knock-on effect on everything else." It could spell disaster.

Mr Kephisto nodded. "It is highly specialised work and wouldn't be trusted to the likes of you and I, Alf."

I frowned at his insinuation—wholly just of course—that I was a bull in a china shop most of the time. Magickal interference would probably not be my strong suit.

"Mmm." I exhaled noisily. "And I would imagine such magick could be open to abuse. If someone wanted to alter time and they managed to get their hands on a member of the order and threaten them with something, bully them, coerce them or whatever…" I trailed off.

"Which is why they are highly secretive, and why your Mr Wylie is so jumpy I imagine."

"So, what did he leave behind at the inn? And why can't he find it?" I ran my hands through my hair. "He seemed desperate."

"That's why you've got to help him if you can, Alf," Mr Kephisto gently reminded me, and I nodded.

"I'll do all I can."

CHAPTER NINE

"Take a seat, love." The desk sergeant indicated some grubby benches behind me. "He'll be down in a minute."

After finishing with Mr Kephisto in Abbotts Cromleigh, I'd hopped on the bus heading into the city of Exeter and then made a change to drop back down towards the coast and Whittlecombe. Jed's van, my current preferred mode of transport, had been left with the garage to have the rear axle attended to. That would be as a result of all the potholes in Devon's roads, no doubt. What was that line in The Beatles' song about holes filling the Albert Hall? The potholes in Devon could fill the Millennium Stadium.

In any case, the lovely mechanics at Whittlecombe Garage had promised to return the van quickly, but probably not till the morning.

The Land Rover I'd taken from Piddlecombe Farm had been returned there a few days before I left on my holidays. I couldn't bear the thought of having The Mori's vehicle anywhere near my beloved wonky inn.

But seeing as I'd found myself in Exeter, I decided to take a detour to the police station where George was most frequently based. I hadn't bothered calling ahead. If he wasn't here if wouldn't matter. It was a simple ten minutes out of my day. I just had a few questions to ask him and it would save him the trip to Whittlecombe if he was busy.

I perched on the bench, watching people as they came and went. Some making enquiries about lost property, others enquiring about making a complaint of one description or another. I listened in, while pretending to study my phone and trying not to giggle, as one woman complained vociferously about her neighbour's cat pooping on her lawn.

I looked up as the door to the side of the counter opened. There was George. He seemed taken aback to see me there. Perhaps the desk sergeant had not passed on my message after all.

"Alf?"

"Hi." I stood with a smile as he sloped towards

me, but my smile froze in place as I saw who was following closely behind him. Stacey.

His 'friend' Stacey from the emergency call centre. Stacey who had helped him to alter his appearance for the Psychic Fayre. Stacey who had taken selfies of the pair of them as she planted a kiss on his cheek. Stacey who had known he had a girl-friend but still pursued him regardless.

I touched the reassuring ancient wood of the wand in my pocket and contemplated turning Stacey into a cockroach but perhaps George read my thoughts because he hurriedly stepped between us.

"Alf!" he repeated. "I wasn't expecting you."

"Obviously," I said and leaned slightly sideways, peering around him so I could scowl at Stacey. She had the decency to blush and turned hurriedly to the desk, to engage the sergeant there in conversation.

"We were just going to grab a bite up the road. Would you like to come?"

The man was crazy. I'd rather have sacrificed my first born to the God of snow and ice—and everyone knows how much I hate snow and ice—than spend time watching Stacey cosy up with 'my' George. Ha!

"No, no. I'm fine thanks," I replied, working on making my tone light and carefree while trying to unclench my teeth. "Dinners to cook, inns to run. You know how it is."

"Always busy." George smiled and took my arm. I resisted the urge to pull away. "How is everyone? Gwyn? Charity? Florence?"

"Very well." I nodded.

"Zephaniah? Luppitt? Monsieur Emietter?"

Was he going to name them all? "Busy. We have a full house at the moment. Monsieur Emietter is concocting a special French supper this evening."

"Oh, lovely."

"A *frogs'* legs starter, I believe." I met George's eye and he blanched slightly.

"Right."

"Right." I repeated and pulled my arm away.

"Alf..." he tried, but I held a hand up.

"Like I said, I can't stay long. I just have a couple of questions for you."

George, looking thoroughly miserable, nodded and folded his arms. "Okay."

"Did you find a cause of death on the skeleton?"

George shook his head. "No. I think we'll be recording an open verdict on that one. We really have nothing to go on. The skeleton is intact with no visible injuries to the bones. There was no damage to the clothing, either, just deterioration of the fabric due to the length of time it had been interred."

"He wasn't killed violently then?"

George shrugged. "That's hard to say. He may have been stabbed—although there is no indication from the clothes that that's the case. And there's nothing to suggest that a knife met a bone. He could have been poisoned. That's a potential line of enquiry, but I think forensic examination of the hair will probably rule that out, too. I think we can also say he wasn't strangled or shot, and he wasn't hung."

"Could he have been bricked up in that space and left to die of starvation?"

George frowned and shook his head. "You do have the slightly macabre imagination of a detective, Alf," he replied with a wry grimace. "Either that or you've been hanging around me too much. I would say that no, he was dead when he was placed there. There's no evidence he tried to claw his way out. No marks on the wall. It's not definite, but it seems unlikely."

That was a relief. I relaxed a little. "And still no identification?"

"No. There was nothing among the bits and pieces we removed from around him that helped us at all." George glanced around to make sure we weren't being listened to, then leaned closer to me. "What about you? Anything you can share?"

"I have a potential lead on who he may be," I replied cagily. "Or I would have, but the person who can help me keeps disappearing."

"Gwyn?"

I rolled my eyes. "I haven't seen her for days, but she's in a right tizz about this whole thing and I'm sure she knows more than she's letting on."

George regarded me with interest. "Someone else then?"

"Yes," I spoke carefully and gave him a meaningful look. "But I can't say any more."

"Alright." He rolled his head back and stared at the ceiling for a moment, then dropped his gaze back to me with those soft blue eyes that I loved. "When you can, you'll fill me in, yeah?"

"I will," I promised.

"Good. We'll get together for another drink soon, shall we?"

I looked over his shoulder at Stacey and curled my lip.

"Alone," he said. "I'll come alone."

CHAPTER TEN

With both Gwyn and Florence missing for the evening dinner service, Charity and I were run off our feet. Although I'd been lying to George when I said I had a full house at the inn —*The Throne Room* was still out of commission after all—we did have plenty of guests to attend to in the aftermath of the bank holiday weekend. Using Finbarr to help with service was out of the question. I needed someone constantly looking to the perimeter of the inn and ensuring the spells used to keep Whittle Inn safe from the attentions of undesirables such as The Mori remained as powerful as when they'd first been cast.

Besides, wherever Finbarr went his pixies invariably followed, and I was in no mood for corralling a bunch of mischievous little miscreants who insisted on running riot around the dining tables and grabbing food from my guests' plates.

Been there, earned that particular badge.

I'd roped in Ned to help behind the bar, so that Zephaniah could help me clear tables and bring out food and drinks, but it wasn't his favourite job. He was an outdoorsy type ghost, was Ned, more at home tending to dahlias and begonias than measures of gin or the proper amount of head allowed on a pint of lager.

At 9.30 pm I left Zephaniah and Ned to look after the bar and sent Charity off duty, too. She looked exhausted, and I felt pretty weary myself. But as I climbed the stairs to my room, I kept going when I reached my landing, up the next flight and the next, until I arrived in the attic, determined to hunt down Florence and Gwyn.

Florence was easy enough to locate. We had converted part of the attic at my father Erik's instigation. He had mentioned to me, quite forcibly as it happened, that eternity is quite a long time, and it gets boring. Given his predilection for playing games on the lawn in the summer, it was no surprise when he suggested a club room of sorts for all of Whittle Inn's ghosts to share.

It had been straightforward enough to create

one. There had been a billiard table in pieces left abandoned in the attic for decades, so I had that put together and the baize recovered. We filled a cupboard with board games, and there were plenty of packs of cards, some that had been around for over a century and shuffled like slices of toast. There were books and crafts, a gramophone and a stereo, and there was a television.

Florence had parked herself in front of the television with the sound down, watching yet another episode of *The Great Witchy Cake-Off*, while many of the other ghosts chattered around her.

"Captain on the deck," Luke Riley, a 1920s sailor announced, and pretended to pipe me aboard. I gave him a look and a few of the other ghosts in our vicinity giggled. Florence however didn't even look up.

"How's it going, Florence?" I called, and walked purposely between her and the television.

"Oh, Miss Alf!" She finally noticed me and quickly jumped up, brushing down her skirts, ash and soot falling towards the ground but evaporating before they could meet the wooden floorboards. I'd heard the expression square-eyed before for people who watch too much TV, but I'd never seen it in practice.

Until today.

I gestured at the television. "Florence, we talked about this."

"I know, Miss." She looked shamefaced. "It's just—"

"Yes?"

"I have so many ideas. I'd love to try them out."

I shrugged. "So try them out, Florence! I've a huge kitchen downstairs and an inn full of hungry supernaturals. Many of them with a sweet tooth. Including me. What's to stop you?"

Florence grimaced. "I'm not sure Monsieur Emietter..."

Ah there it was in a nutshell. Monsieur Emietter had always been a tyrant in the kitchen, although truth to tell he had a heart of gold. The problems arose because he didn't speak English and nobody at the inn spoke any French.

Apart from Gwyn and she was absent more than she was present at times.

I sighed. "Florence, my dear. This is *my* inn. *My* kitchen." I paused, knowing that if Gwyn were around, she'd have corrected me. The inn wasn't mine, it was simply in my care. I was custodian of the bricks and the mortar, of the grounds and the woods, but more importantly the spirits and other creatures and the magickal essence that breathed life into us all. "Well you know what I mean," I said. "I'll tell Monsieur Emietter that you're allowed cake-baking time."

"And bread?" Florence asked.

"Of course." Florence's bread was exceptional.

"And pies?"

"Well okay." That would probably involve treading a little more on my French chef's toes.

"And puddings."

"I'll see what I can do, Florence," I promised and hurried away before she made poor Monsieur Emietter redundant.

A cursory glance of the attic room proved Gwyn's absence, so I tried the room on the other side of the attic stairs. I flicked the light switch, illuminating a smaller room. It smelled slightly musty. Motes of dust floated in the air. This was where the old records for the inn were kept, many arranged neatly on bookshelves and others piled high in cardboard boxes. Old accounts, receipts, signing in and visitor books, customer records, invoices—you name it—anything that pre-dated the age of the computer database were all stored here somewhat haphazardly.

But no sign of Gwyn.

I was about to exit and make my way back downstairs when a thought occurred to me.

The entries on my computer records with regard to Mr Wylie had been erased. I wasn't sure that Gwyn had done it, but her magick was powerful enough that she could have done, even without knowing little about modern day software.

But would she have bothered to erase any hard copy evidence of his stay at the inn?

Even if she had, any irregularity would be noticeable. Without destroying all the records, a smudged entry or a torn-out page was going to aid in the identification of when Mr Wylie may have stayed at the inn in the past. This might help me find out more information both about Mr Wylie and his friend.

I gazed with distaste at the books in front of me. There were hundreds of them. Proper record keeping at the inn had been started by my Victorian ancestors, not surprising given that the Victorians as a society had been obsessed with record keeping and data, and my forebears were no exception. From the 1840s the records were highly detailed and recorded in a neat legible hand. Most of the nineteenth century record books were black leather. From 1902 they were oxblood red until 1940 when they became green. Prior to the 1840s the books were brick coloured, the paper edges now dry and crumbling with age.

I groaned. This would be like finding a needle in a haystack.

It seemed like a good idea but for now I decided to sleep on it.

Funny how your subconscious likes to work out all your problems for you while you sleep.

I jolted awake in the early hours and sat bolt upright. The obvious place to start looking through the registers would be to line up my investigation with the date on the back of the photo that George had shown me. He'd given me a copy of the photo, not the original, but while asleep I'd remembered the date.

I scrambled out of bed and slipped through to my office, scrabbling around on the desk for a pen and paper. Switching the desk lamp on, I scrawled the date to remind myself to check in the morning.

Then I stumbled back to bed and fell deeply asleep once more.

After that, my dreams were weird. George, Stacey and I were floating around in space, struggling to stay together without gravity to help us. Mr Wylie was there, and he was crying because he had lost something. I kept asking him what he'd lost, but he wouldn't tell me. Then Florence floated up into space to join us—easy for her given her ghostly form and the fact she was accustomed to floating everywhere. She offered us all a cupcake, but when I took a bite of mine I found it was covered in feathers.

"Does Mr Hoo know you have his feathers?" I asked Florence, but she was too busy watching television to answer me, her eyes were squares, which reflected the stars around us.

I woke up with a start, imagining I was spitting feathers out of my mouth. Mr Hoo backed slowly away from me and settled on the arm of the window.

"Hooo-oooo," he told me. "Hooo!"

"You're right," I answered. "I'm cracking up."

As I'd suspected, Gwyn had not altered the original records.

An entry for Mr William Wylie existed for the dates July 18th, 1920 through July 25th inclusive. The entry had been made in black ink, in the same handwriting I'd seen on the reverse of the photo. A small neat cursive hand. Gwyn's most likely.

The same handwriting had filled in hundreds and hundreds of entries in this reservation book. Under her patronage, Whittle Inn had been a popular haunt—excuse the pun. I ran my finger along the page of entries feeling oddly melancholy. She'd been so very alive when she'd completed the details contained here. Laughing, loving, talking, eating, walking on the ground, sleeping, brushing her hair—just being physical.

"Oh, Grandmama," I muttered, feeling sad for her, although I knew she would hate me being maudlin for her sake. She'd often told me she enjoyed her spirit existence, so I shouldn't have minded it on her behalf.

William Wylie had been staying in what had then been Room 4. When I'd taken over the inn, the rooms had been relabelled according to the floor they were on, so I couldn't be sure exactly which one had been Room 4. However, I figured that logically it would be one of the bedrooms on the same floor as my suite of rooms so that Room 4 subsequently became Room 104 and then *The Throne Room* after I'd made my own changes.

Directly underneath William Wylie's entry was

another that could only refer to the 'GG' of the photo. This entry belonged to Guillaume Gorde. He'd been placed in Room 3. Both of them had given their address as care of *The Full Moon* on Celestine Street. That was standard among witches who didn't want to be tracked down, I knew that. However, I was surprised that Gwyn had allowed them to register only using those details.

Why had she felt those two deserved a special treatment?

Could I make the assumption that Guillaume Gorde was William Wylie's lost friend? Was he the skeleton behind the wall? Or had Mr Wylie stayed at the inn on any other occasion and with other friends? Flicking through every entry in every book in the attic store was going to take me ages.

Unless...

A vision of Mr Kephisto and the way he had located information the day before materialised in my mind. Could I use my magick, too?

I ran my fingers along the spines of the black leather volumes leaving a clean trail in the dust, grey fluff bunching up on the tip of my finger. Florence obviously didn't get in here much, but then I'd never asked her to do so.

Nothing jumped out at me. The books continued

to appear normal, nothing out of the ordinary. The books in Mr Kephisto's room had positively glowed with a vibrant and unmistakeable force.

I blew on the dust on my finger. "*Animare.*" I breathed the word, softly, and watched as the sprinkles scattered in the air, floating gently on my breath. For a moment it didn't appear that anything would happen, and then suddenly each speck began to glow as though a miniature fire had been set within. The burning specks drifted towards the books and finally lit the torch paper. A rapid pulse of energy spread through them, from the black volumes to those with oxblood leather and then on to the green.

Now when I ran my finger along the side of the books, they glittered underneath my touch. "*Ostendus,*" I ordered, "Mr William Wylie." I watched in satisfaction as one black-spined volume, and then another, followed by one oxblood and another, and then no less than four tattered green volumes pushed their way out from the wall.

I plucked the volumes out and created a pile. This made my job so much easier.

In between the other tasks and chores needing attention, I pored over the volumes on my desk in the office where the light was better for scrutinising the faded entries in the books. I kept half an eye out for Gwyn in case she appeared somewhere. There were so many questions I wanted to ask her, but she continued to remain hidden from me.

The process of searching through entry after entry in each ledger took hours. At first, when I drew a blank, I imagined my magick hadn't pulled out the correct volumes at all, but eventually towards the back of the first book I spotted the first entry for William Wylie. He'd first stayed at the inn, according to the records at any rate, on 27th April 1888 for two days. Alone.

By the end of the day, when my eyes were tired and scratchy, I had a list of dates that a William Wylie had stayed at the inn, and a shorter list for Guilluame Gorde. Gorde had only ever stayed at the same time as Mr Wylie, but the last occasion they had stayed together had been 1932.

Mr Wylie had subsequently stayed at the inn twenty-four more times according to the paper records. Most noticeably five times in 1942 and seven times in 1983.

So, what kept bringing him back?

I rubbed my eyes and stared at the list in front of

me. I had no way of conjuring up Mr Wylie myself. He came, he went, and I didn't know how.

I couldn't track down Gwyn—she was nowhere to be found, and none of the other ghosts were able to tell me where she was hiding.

Mr Kephisto had helped me as much as he could.

George couldn't do magick.

And besides... he had Stacey. Ugh.

The skeleton—Guillaume Gorde I assumed—had left his mortal remains in the gap in the wall, and a few material bits and pieces, but he hadn't left his ghost light, so I wasn't able to call him to me and ask what had happened to him and how he'd ended up incarcerated at the inn.

I needed somebody who could communicate with the dead after they had crossed over. A necromancer.

I knew just the man.

The problem was, I had no easy way to contact him.

CHAPTER ELEVEN

September in the countryside is one thing—even in poor weather the Devon landscape never seems greener nor more alive than in the weeks before Autumn sets in. In Speckled Wood, recovering well now after the toxic outbreak that had nearly killed it, small mammals—badgers, foxes, squirrels, moles, voles, mice and hares—were busy making initial preparations for the winter ahead. They lived each day as if it was their last. The trees reached for the sun at every opportunity. Late flowers and early berries bloomed bright and ripe, fed by the rain and the sunlight in equal measure, and enticed all comers.

September in the city, on a rainy day, well that's something else.

The shop windows on Celestial Street glowed with their usual warmth, while the cobbles, slick with rain, sparkled in the light. The heavenly scent of pies and sweet treats filled the air, but today—as I had once before—I was turning to the dark side.

Pulling my hood over my head, I hurried down Cross Lane. The narrow thoroughfare separated the shining and happy Celestial Street; where witches, wizards, sages and mages came to undertake their business all legally and above board, from the underbelly of our magickal world. Here in the back alleys, the disenfranchised and the dark, the excluded and the forgotten, the heavy of heart and the doers of black deeds, lived in tiny cramped lodgings. Anonymity was treasured here. Payments were made in cash and upfront. Visitors were expected to forget all they'd witnessed as soon as they vacated the area.

The first time I'd hired Horace T Silvanus, it had taken me several weeks to make the right connections and had cost me a small fortune in a down payment. Silvan, as I now knew him, was a highly secretive individual who earned his living as a wizard-for-hire, a conductor of dirty activities, who could be trusted to get in, do a job, and get out again and then keep his mouth firmly shut. He lived on the wrong side of the tracks because that was his preference. I'd hired him to help me learn the dark arts and become a better fighting witch.

So here I was again, approaching *The Web and Flame*, with my fingers crossed that I'd find Silvan inside.

As if it would be that easy.

The *Web and Flame* was exactly as I remembered it. White-washed walls and small fires burning in black grates that gave off no warmth or cheer. There were a few small gatherings of solemn folks, conducting business in hushed tones, and a number of solitary individuals sitting at the rough wooden table, staring into the bottom of their tankards, or reading newspapers.

On the face of it, nobody paid me any mind, but I was no naïve witch anymore. The old Alfhild Daemonne might have assumed she could travel incognito and talk her way out of any situation but having trained closely with Silvan in the weeks leading up to finding George, having fought The Mori on more than one occasion, and having come close to losing almost everything I held dear, I was no longer that foolish girl.

My wits remained on high alert. I rebuffed any curious advances that came my way—slapped away the enquiring thought tentacles sent out by silent observers attempting to inveigle their way into my mind. Simultaneously I sent out my own and was just as quickly repulsed.

While the toothless and bald man behind the bar was familiar to me—he'd been the landlord I'd seen in here before—there was no spark of recognition in his eyes. He stood in front of his optics, polishing glasses with a soiled cloth. I laid some coins on his counter. "A glass of *Hoodwinker*, please."

The landlord set his lips into a thin line and dawdled across to his pumps to pull me a short measure. I didn't complain. I wouldn't be drinking the ale on this occasion anyway. When he plonked the glass down in front of me, I covered the coins with my hand.

"Would you know the whereabouts of Silvan?" I asked, absolutely certain that everyone would know everyone else in this tiny backwater of the magickal world. Infamy and daring deeds had to amount for something.

The landlord's eyes remained black, the look on his face distinctly disinterested.

"No," he replied shortly. "No idea who you mean."

It didn't matter. It was enough.

I carried my glass to a free table and sat with my

back against the wall so that I could watch people coming and going. I didn't have to wait long before I spotted a small girl dart out of the front entrance and turn left, heading further down Knick-Knack Lane and away from Cross Lane.

My message would be delivered.

I took a quick swig of my *Hoodwinker*. It was as good as I remembered. An ale remarkably dark and rich in colour, but which tasted light and refreshing. Whatever else you might say about *The Web and Flame*, the beers were top-notch.

After a few minutes, I abandoned my drink and exited the pub. The rain was falling straight like stair-rods, leaking relentlessly from a miserable and sour-grey sky. Water dripped down the walls of the old buildings or trickled from ancient iron guttering. I turned left and walked along Knick-Knack Lane, further into the underworld than I had ever ventured before.

I was entering a rabbit warren of epic proportions; it would be easy to get lost. I kept half an eye on potential landmarks: a teeny bakery, a pie shop, an old wand shop—this latter little more than a window into someone else's front room—a magickal curios shop and several more public houses and inns. At the same time, I envisaged a gold thread unravelling around the streets and lanes and thoroughfares as I walked. I would use this to find my way back.

The little girl had disappeared from view, but again that wasn't important. As long as the message had been delivered, I trusted everything else would go to plan. I continued onward, making sure to mentally note the street signs where they were visible.

It was therefore disappointing, thirty-five minutes later, to find myself back in Knick-Knack Lane, very close to *The Web and Flame.* I stopped stock still and glared at the old inn in front of me. How had I managed that?

Then the little girl stepped right out in front of me, so close I could have almost touched her. She gazed up at me through large dark eyes, her face, streaked with dirt, but with no expression at all. With a small movement of her head, she indicated a door to the right of her and took to her heels, disappearing into the entrance of *The Web and Flame.*

I watched her go, and then with one last glance along the street I turned to my left to duck through the doorway she'd indicated. A narrow and steep flight of old wooden stairs led up to a landing, a kind of open veranda looking down onto the street below.

A second entrance took me up more stairs to the next level.

A pair of louvre doors were propped open in front of me. I carefully approached them and peered through. A woman of about my age with long white hair was pulling a jacket over her thin bodice. She spotted me and smiled, beckoning me through. The room was surprisingly light, painted white, with pot plants dotted around and three wicker chairs grouped around a glass table, each of them draped with orange throws.

"Out the back there," she said, indicating another room through a wooden beaded curtain. She bent to retrieve a small hessian sack and disappeared through the louvre doors. I walked through to the back room.

The blinds had been drawn in here and it took my eyes a moment to adjust to the darkness, but when I could finally focus, I was thankful to see Silvan lounging on his bed watching me.

"Alfhild Daemonne, as I live and breathe." I'd grown accustomed to his drawl, and his handsome face. In fact, he had become so familiar, and such a part of my adventures with The Mori, that seeing him again was rather like looking in a mirror.

My stomach fluttered with a sudden onset of

nerves. "If I'd known you lived so close to *The Web and Flame* it would have saved me a whole lot of shoe leather," I complained.

"Oh, I don't live here. This is Marissa's place." He nodded towards the door and the white-haired woman who had left us to it.

"Is that your girlfriend?" I asked. He'd never mentioned a partner before, and I found myself curious.

"One of many," he smirked at me. When I rolled my eyes, he laughed. "And how is your beau? The brave and intrepid DS Gilchrist? I trust he's recovered from him time spent in the marshes of Speckled Wood?"

"I didn't leave him there for very long, you know that," I chastised Silvan. "And he's not my beau." I averted my gaze so he couldn't see any residue of pain there. "Not anymore."

Silvan was quiet for a moment. "I see. I'm sorry."

Silvan didn't *do* sorry, so I took that with a pinch of salt.

He rolled out of bed and stood, wrapping the coverlet around himself. "So what brings you here? You're not in trouble, are you?"

I averted my gaze while he collected his clothes together.

"No. Not really."

"Not really?"

"Back at the inn, we found a skeleton in the walls. To cut a long story short, it seems that it's been there for some time, although we haven't been able to put a date to it. I think Gwyn knows something about who it is and where it came from, but she won't talk about it."

Silvan started to pull his clothes on. "Okay. But why should that concern me? Why come all the way up here?"

Good question. "I'm not entirely sure. It's bothering me. I mean... how this fellow came to meet his end. And... I'm worried that someone in my family may have been involved..."

"And because you're such a goody-two-shoes you don't like that idea."

I narrowed my eyes at him. "Well of course I don't."

"Same old, Alfhild. Still trying to save the world, eh?" Silvan laughed and buttoned up his black tunic.

I bristled. "I don't think that's what I'm trying to do. It's just a mystery I want to solve, and I thought you might be able to help me."

Silvan dropped back down on to the bed and

pulled on a long black leather boot and set about lacing it up as I moved around to face him.

"What's in it for me?" he asked.

That stung, too. "I thought we were friends. I thought..."

"You think too much." Silvan reached for his wand on the bedside table and jabbed at somewhere behind me. His hat soared through the air, narrowly missing my shoulder. He caught it with his free hand and placed it on his head at a jaunty angle.

"Shall we grab a spot of lunch?" he asked, and pointed at the door. "You can tell me all about it."

"I suppose so," I harrumphed. The man was impossible.

"Your treat," he said, and bowed me out of the room.

Seven hours later we were back in Devon. Silvan had been surprisingly easy to persuade to return to the inn with me. I'd shown him to the room he'd stayed in before, it was small and plain, but he seemed to like it. Then I'd offered him some dinner, but he'd insisted he wanted to have a look inside *The Throne Room* first.

"How interesting," he'd exclaimed as I followed him in. He poked his head into the gap between the walls and scanned the area, cocking his head and listening. Finally, he pulled out some chalk from his pocket and enclosed the secret space within two semi-circles. He drew a number of symbols between the two lines.

"Take me through to the room next door. Is anyone staying there?"

"No," I said, showing him the way. "We can't really use these rooms until we've completed the work we started."

"Lucky for us then." By feeling the wall on this side, he was able to locate the start and finish of the semi-circles next door and join them up.

We returned to *The Throne Room* and I watched again, feeling slightly useless as well as curious. He knelt in the gap between the walls in the location where we had discovered the skeleton, then ran his hands lightly around the floor, not touching anything. I watched his fingers quiver in certain places, and then he stood and repeated the process close to the remaining walls and into the cavity above his head.

He dropped into a squat again and began murmuring, speaking the words of a spell I didn't know or understand. I kept quiet, minding my own business. It wasn't my place to interfere.

Finally, he finished what he was doing, brought his hands together in a quiet gesture of thanks and stepped out of the circle.

"Interesting." His black eyes sparkled. "What haven't you told me?"

"What do you mean?" It wasn't my intention to be cagey, I just wasn't sure what he needed to know.

Silvan reached for my arm and pulled me close to the hole in the wall. "Put your hand up," he said, directing me to hold my hand in mid-air, about six inches in front of the right-hand corner. "What do you feel?"

I ran my palm back and forth without touching the wall. "Nothing," I said finally, disappointed that I couldn't sense anything, not in the way that he could.

"Alright." Silvan pushed my arm down, about three feet above the floorboards. "And now?"

At first, I felt nothing, but then as I moved my hand slightly left and then right again, I sensed it. A slight magickal frisson.

"What is that?"

Silvan knelt next to the hole and I followed suit, my hand following his, creating a trail, like a large rectangle. "It's a forcefield. I can't be sure, because the traces are so faint, but I reckon it's a repellent."

"To stop people getting into this space?" I asked.

Silvan shrugged. "Perhaps to stop anyone knowing about it."

"It was so well hidden..."

"Yes. But think about it. This is a public place run by supernaturals. It stands to reason that other supernaturals might have sensed something between the walls and have been curious about it. By putting a repelling force in place, they could keep anyone curious at bay."

That kind of made sense. "Well who do you mean by 'they'? Someone was pretty determined the body should never be found, that's for sure." A deep sense of unease shifted within me.

Silvan grunted. "Somebody who didn't think it through."

"What do you mean?"

Silvan squatted back on his heels, frowning. "Look, whoever set this forcefield up, they knew their way around magick alright. This is good strong advanced magick."

I could see the 'but' coming a mile off.

"But it's the sort of magick a good witch would perform." I instantly knew where this was going.

Silvan had repeated this many a time. "A devious mind would know that a repelling forcefield will attract its own share of interest." He smiled at me. "Believe me, when I see a sign that tells me to 'keep out or not to enter, it acts like a red rag to a bull. It's green for go. I'm straight in there."

He waved his hand around the hole again. "For sure, not everyone can pick up on traces of magickal energy—you couldn't do it particularly well until I trained you for example. But there are many of us who can, and some of us would find such a forcefield worth exploring."

He laughed, but without humour. "To be honest, the creator of this forcefield was doing the best they could at the time, but I think it backfired."

I didn't understand what he was driving at. "Why do you say that?"

"Because this forcefield wasn't destroyed by your builders. It had already been disrupted prior to that. Someone else had been in here."

"But you'd never have known that from the state of the wall," I protested.

Silvan inhaled noisily and considered that. "It must have been some time ago then."

"I guess so."

"You said you had some photos of the body in place when it was discovered?"

"Yes, George gave me copies."

"Show me."

I slipped back to the office and rummaged among the folders in my bottom drawer until I found the envelope George had passed to me. I bought them back to Silvan, finding him sitting against the wall by the door, staring into the hole, a faraway look in his eyes.

"Here they are." I offered the images to him. He spent a few minutes examining them, not saying anything.

He turned one of the photos towards me. The one with the robes. "What did you say this order were called?"

"The Cosmic Order of Chronometric Wizards." I'd told him what I had discovered over lunch in *The Web and Flame*—where incidentally the food was as good as the beer.

"Oh, that's right. Clever." He'd enthused about an order of wizards that could travel through time. "I bet they'd have some serious skills I'd like to learn more about."

He took the photo from me and handed me the next one. The skeleton sitting upright in the corner, hands in his lap, personal items scattered around him. "So, I've got good news and bad news."

"Go on."

He tapped the photo. "The good news is… I don't think your victim here was murdered. So, if one of your ancestors was involved in the interment, I don't think they were a murderer."

I looked at him askance. "Well that is good news, but how can you tell?"

"Look." Silvan pointed at the body. "Look at the way the body has been arranged."

"He's on display," I said. "Don't murderers do that?"

"Sure they do, but I wouldn't say he was on display. In fact, I'd argue that he'd been arranged with great compassion. He's sitting up, his hands are in his lap. He'd been left there holding a book and he had his belongings with him. That doesn't sound to me like someone was trying to hide a crime. It feels more respectful somehow."

I shook my head, unsure. "That's difficult to prove," I challenged.

"What are you? A high court judge? Okay it's a guess, but it's an informed one."

"Can't you ask him?" Isn't that what necromancers were supposed to be able to do? Communicate with the dead?

"That's the bad news. The scene has been cleansed very thoroughly."

"The police came and did their thing," I said.

"Old Georgie?"

"Well him and his team. They took everything away."

"All the evidence left with the body you mean? Physical and tangible evidence. No, when I say cleansed, I mean it was more than that. This area has been magickly cleansed. I can't get a fix on this man at all. Who he was and what he did. Nothing. Not even how he died. Somebody with powerful abilities. Who would do that if it wasn't you?"

"It definitely wasn't me." I thought about the people who'd enjoyed access to the room. "Well Gwyn, I suppose." The thought troubled me. Why was Gwyn working so hard to hide any evidence relating to the identity of the skeleton and the reason for his death?

"Could she have done that? Impressive. Our next step should involve locating your great-grandmother and having a word with her."

"I wish we could," I replied. Then a logical thought struck me. "But there's someone else who had access to this room, isn't there? I told you about him. Mr Wylie? I'm willing to bet his magick is unlike anything we've seen before."

"I want to go back up to the room." Silvan appeared troubled.

We'd been tucking into a late supper of cold cuts teamed with potato salad, along with a beetroot and onion relish, and the tail end of the day's freshly baked bread. Silvan as always had a healthy appetite, but unusually he had refused the bottle of beer I'd offered to go with the meal. We were eating alone at the kitchen table. Charity had disappeared up to her room, and although Florence had apparently been attending to her duties at some stage, she too was nowhere in sight and I could only assume she was catching up on her fix of television in the games room in the attic. I had Zephaniah and Ned on the bar.

"Okay." I placed my knife and fork neatly in the centre of my plate. "Now?"

"I need an artefact."

"An artefact? What kind of artefact?"

Silvan smiled, his face grim. "From the body."

I chose to misconstrue his meaning deliberately. "Oh. You mean... like his clothes? Or one of the original photos? The book?"

With a shake of his head, Silvan slid his dinner plate into the centre of the table. "No. It needs to be more personal than that. I need something directly from the body, like hair, or skin. A bone would be better."

I baulked at this. "A bone? From the body? How are we going to be able to get that?"

Silvan gave me a pointed look. "Your friend George, of course."

"You want what?"

"Hahaha." I laughed to cover my nerves. The last thing I wanted to be doing was calling George for help at this time of night. "Yes, it is a strange request admittedly. But we do need it, otherwise I wouldn't ask."

"I should put the phone down right now, Alf. You're crazy." George sounded cross and more than a little weary himself. "What are you going to use it for?"

I hesitated. "It's not for me. Well, not really.

Silvan is here. He's going to try and communicate with whomever was in that gap in the wall."

There was a heavy silence that went on for far too long, until I heard someone call George's name.

That Stacey woman.

I bristled. Boy, she had moved quickly.

"Silvan is there with you, is he?" George asked, his tone hardening.

"Just as Stacey is there with *you*," I retorted.

Another silence. I took a deep breath and calmed myself. I could imagine the wheels of George's mind turning.

"Look, let's discuss it in the morning, shall we? I can't imagine how much paperwork I'd have to fill in to remove a bone from the mortuary even if the coroner would agree."

Oh dear. He wouldn't like what was coming next. I steeled myself. "Erm... yeah. We need it here at the inn by midnight." I winced and waited for the explosion.

"You're out of your mind," George replied calmly, and the phone went dead.

I removed the phone from my ear and studied the screen. *Call ended.* I grimaced.

"That didn't go to plan, I take it?" Silvan asked, raising an amused eyebrow.

"About as well as you'd expect. What do we do now?"

Silvan slid his chair back and stood. "Get your shoes on. Grab the van keys. We're going out."

I sighed in exasperation, tired out after my early start and return trip to London. Where did Silvan get his energy from? "Where are we going?"

Silvan was already moving. "We're going to meet George. He'll be ringing you back any second."

How could he possibly know that? Reluctantly, I reached for the boots I'd taken off and discarded under the table. Were we really heading out on a wild goose chase at this time of night?

It turned out we were. I'd hardly finished lacing my boots when my mobile rang.

Silvan and I, in Jed's newly-fixed old van, drove across the moor towards Exeter and pulled into a rough clearing that passed as a car park just before 11 p.m. George lived in Exeter, near the main police station, and so it had seemed simplest to meet him halfway.

"How did you know he would change his mind?" I asked Silvan, as we sat in the van and waited for

George to show up. My stomach twanged with anxiety and I fidgeted with my keys. What we were asking George to do wasn't legal. He could end up in serious hot water.

Silvan shrugged. "He's an honourable man. He owes us for saving his life."

I frowned. "Poor George. He wouldn't have ended up needing our help if I hadn't involved him in my struggle in the first place."

"That's life," Silvan replied, closing his eyes and slouching further into his seat. I turned my head sideways to stare at him. Did he care about anyone except himself?

Headlights beamed in the distance, coming over the brow of a hill, alerting me to another vehicle. George's battered silver Audi indicated to enter the car park, and he pulled up opposite us. I nudged Silvan, although he must have heard the noise of the other car joining us, and he jumped to attention.

Like two outlaw gangs of cowboys meeting head-on in the Wild West, George and Stacey and Silvan and I met in the middle of the car park.

Silvan regarded Stacey with interest and tipped his hat at her. "Pleased to meet you," he drawled and offered his hand. George narrowed his eyes at Silvan, as I inwardly seethed. What did this Stacey woman have, that I didn't? Sure, she was pretty enough. Slim, dark hair, almond eyes, clear complexion. Obviously, the men doted on her. But... hello? What about conniving, manipulative and a man-eater?

I felt a snarl building in my throat.

You've either got it or you haven't, Alf, I told myself, *but never you mind. There are always bigger fish to fry.*

"This is Stacey," I told Silvan, but he already knew that of course. He glanced at me with a knowing smirk. I badly wanted to kick his shins. "And this is Silvan," I told her and elected to leave it at that. If George wanted to explain who and what Silvan was, that would be up to him.

"I have what you asked for." George held up a plastic evidence bag with a small white bone inside.

"Ah perfect," Silvan purred and accepted it from him. "A proximal phalange."

"I hope getting hold of it didn't cause too much trouble?" I asked, worried about the potential consequences for everyone involved.

George seemed stoic. "Not the easiest night at the office." He turned to Silvan. "I need it back. First thing in the morning."

"Just come with us now," Silvan grinned. "Join in our merry gathering. You might find it interesting."

George gazed at Silvan in horror. "No thanks. I'll give that a wide berth. In recent months I've had enough *interesting* experiences to last me for quite some time."

Stacey looked on curiously, not saying a word. Her face didn't give much away. I wondered how much she knew and what she was thinking.

"I'll be outside the inn at six tomorrow morning. I need to get the bone back to the morgue before seven." George looked at me pointedly. "Don't make me regret this."

"We won't," I promised. "I'll share with you anything we find out tonight."

"I can't wait," George said and spun on his heel, heading back to his car. Stacey paused, smiling at Silvan, with what looked like open admiration, then she too turned away and slunk back to the Audi.

Silvan watched her for longer than he should have, so I reached out and tugged at his sleeve.

"Come on," I grumbled. "Time's ticking on."

Silvan laughed. "Oh, those green eyes of yours, Alfhild. See how they shine."

At midnight, everything was ready.

We'd magickly sealed *The Throne Room*, windows and doors, so that if Silvan managed to conjure up the spirit of the departed, they could be held in place without fear of losing them. Silvan had re-chalked the floor with a double circle, and carefully but hurriedly filled the space in between with symbols and marks that obviously meant something to him. He'd arranged the phalange in the centre, surrounded by unlit candles, scattered dirt from one of the flowerbeds in the grounds to symbolise earth, a goblet of water, and incense and feathers to represent air. With all the elemental bases covered, he was ready to make a start at midnight.

"You know I've never done anything like this?" I whispered. The atmosphere in the room had changed, becoming solemn.

Silvan patted my arm reassuringly. "You won't have to do anything. Stay calm and quiet and observe. The chances are the spirit won't even see you. The dialogue will be between me and him."

"Alright," I breathed. Moving to the edge of the room, I sank to the floor and sat cross-legged. I would see everything that would happen while remaining safely out of the way.

As the distant sound of the inn's ancient Grandfather clock began to chime downstairs, I observed as

Silvan drew himself up very tall, breathing into his diaphragm. His feet were bare, and he had dressed simply in a long black robe. Now he squatted down on his haunches, both hands clenched to his chest. As the chimes of midnight died away, I watched him flick his fingers and shoot fire into the centre of the circle. The candles burst into life.

Silvan drew his hands together once more as though they contained a small ball.

"Gentle spirit who passed from one life to the next in this place," he intoned. "Here am I, Horace Tiberius Silvanus, seeking an audience with you and you alone. Come to me, only if it pleases you, and if it pleases the gods and goddesses whom we both deign to serve." Silvan parted his hands, widened the circle and stared into the space between them.

The candles gutted and flickered, casting moving shadows around the walls. A whisper of a breeze brushed against my cheek and the air pressure in the room changed. I sensed we were no longer alone. My eyes skipped along the walls and scrutinized the shadows.

Silvan widened his hands further and a spark from one of the candles spat into the air, exploding in a golden ribbon of light. The ribbon darted left and right then up and down, an out-of-control electric eel. Moving swiftly, it elongated itself in every direction and grew to encompass a large area in the gap between the wall as though the hand of an invisible man was tying a parcel with the light from a sparkler. Silvan had uncovered a forcefield of some kind. One that had once shielded a body secretly within its confines.

Silvan held his hands up, flat against the energy field. "Let me talk to you," he asked again, pushing into the current. I could imagine how that felt—like squeezing against a prickly mattress, soft but not altogether yielding.

The gold shimmered for a moment, sparkling with vibrant life until a dark thread appeared, growing blacker, deepening as it ran down the front of the forcefield, and widening until it was about six inches wide.

A candle flickered once more, and a shadow passed beyond the gap. A pale face. Silvan reached forwards, thrust his hand into the area beyond and I gazed in wonder as a pale hand reached to take Silvan's. Thin fingers—almost transparent—curled around Silvan's own.

"Well met," said Silvan. "But I'm struggling to hear you. Can you—"

The forcefield in front of Silvan suddenly stuttered. From somewhere deep within came a flash of vibrant red that flooded *The Throne Room* with a strange light. A second later a fierce wind blew the candles out and we were plunged into darkness. I heard Silvan thrashing around and cursing as the forcefield wavered once, twice, then died away altogether. "Get the lights," he called, and I quickly pushed myself to standing and swept my hands along the wall till I came to the door and located the light switches.

With the room bathed in light once more, all evidence of the forcefield had disappeared. Silvan was brushing dirt from his hands.

"What happened?" I asked. "I thought you'd connected."

"I definitely had. That's quite some forcefield in place there. Powerful, powerful magick. An old magick." He gazed in wonder at where it had been and reached out as though he could still feel it. "But did you see the rent in the energy?"

"I did."

"It allowed me access, for just a fraction of time."

I padded over to Silvan and knelt beside him, holding my hands out and feeling for the faint pulse of energy. "It's a shame it wasn't just a little bit longer. We could have found out who he was and how he died."

Silvan smiled. "Give me some credit, please."

"You know?" I gaped at Silvan in surprise. "But there was hardly any time."

"I don't need much time. His touch was enough." Silvan stood and offered me his hand. I took it and he pulled me to my feet. His hands were warm, the skin slightly dry. A frisson of energy passed between us, some residue perhaps of the forcefield in the room. "I found out some interesting facts."

"Go on." I removed my hand and the small electric tremor dissipated.

"You were right in your supposition. This gentleman *was* called Guillaume Gorde and he *was* a member of the Cosmic Order of Chronometric Wizards."

That much we'd guessed but it was good to hear confirmation.

"Do you know when he died?" I asked.

"No. The strength of that forcefield prevented me from finding that out. But the forcefield itself is interesting."

"How so?"

"That tear we saw? That was far more recent than the forcefield itself."

"You could tell?"

"Oh definitely. One was old magick, the other was more recent."

"Well how recent? I mean, since the body was discovered? Maybe it was us? Maybe we disturbed something when we found him?"

Silvan shook his head and stroked his chin. "I might have thought that, but no, for sure the interference was newer than the magick from when Guillaume was interred, but not the last few weeks. Not even the last few years. Maybe a couple of decades old."

"Ugh." I leaned back against the wall and rubbed my eyes. They were gritty from lack of sleep. "What are you saying? Guillaume was interred in the wall cavity quite some time ago—"

"Over a hundred years ago, I'd say."

"And then someone discovered him before us? And managed to get through the forcefield?"

"That's pretty much the long and the short of it. They patched up the forcefield so that the body wasn't discovered by the next witch who stayed in this room. Not a great job but good enough."

I looked around the room. What had gone on in here?

"Why would somebody do that? Why wouldn't

they have told..." I searched through what I knew of my family history. How many years were we talking? Thirty? Forty? "Why wouldn't they have told my grandparents? Were they covering up a murder?"

Silvan shook his head. "Well that brings me to the most interesting thing I discovered."

I waited expectantly and Silvan smiled devilishly.

"Guillaume almost certainly wasn't murdered. He died from natural causes."

CHAPTER TWELVE

I rolled over in disbelief when my alarm went off the next morning. Without taking my lavender eye-mask off—a gift from Millicent when I started having trouble sleeping a few months before—I fumbled blindly around for my mobile phone on the bedside table.

"I've been asleep for about five minutes," I grumbled. "No way is it tomorrow yet."

"You always did have problems waking up, Alfhild." The familiar voice of my dearly-departed great-grandmother startled me properly into consciousness. I peeled the eye mask off in a hurry and sat up.

"Grandmama?"

"Good morning, my dear." She hovered at the foot of the bed, one hand above Mr Hoo's head. He looked mighty pleased with himself for some reason.

"Where have you been?" I yanked my duvet sideways and thrust my legs over the edge of the bed. "I've been trying to track you down."

Gwyn shrugged the first part of my question off. "I appreciate that, Alfhild, but I..." She paused, her face crumbling. I had never seen my stern and straight-laced great-grandmother in pain before and it took me by surprise. I reached out to her, wishing, not for the first time that I could touch her and reassure her. The lack of physical sensation was by far the worst thing about my gift to see ghosts.

"Grandmama?" I cried, and Mr Hoo swivelled his head around to twit-twoo at her.

Gwyn waved her hands at me and then at him. "I'm fine. It's fine, my dear. Don't worry."

Clearly it wasn't.

"What can I do? How can I help you?" I asked. "Is this about Guillaume?"

Fat tears ran down my great-grandmother's face. "You know about him?"

"I've been doing a bit of digging through the records. I looked at the paper records in the attic." Gwyn nodded. "And Silvan is here. Last night he tried to connect with—" I drew my breath in sharply. "What time is it?" I plucked my phone from the bedside table. Just after six.

"George!" I shrieked and flew out of the room, running down the corridor in my pyjamas and bare feet, to *The Throne Room.* I burst in. The candles and debris from the previous evening lay where they had been discarded, but Guillaume's proximal phalange had disappeared.

Squeaking with worry I took to my heels again, pounding up the stairs, two flights, to the top floor and the room where Silvan slept.

Charity was just coming out of her room, freshly showered, ready to get started with the breakfast service. "Everything okay?" she asked, clearly surprised to see me in my pyjamas standing outside Silvan's room.

"Yes, yes, fine. I'll be down in a minute," I told her.

"Make sure you get dressed first," she replied archly and tittered as she made her way downstairs.

I hammered sharply on Silvan's door again and when there was still no reply, burst in.

He lay on his side in his bed, staring at me in evident amusement.

"Guillaume's phalange? I can't find it."

"Steady those horses, Alfhild. It's all been taken care of."

"George—"

"Has been and gone." I opened my mouth and Silvan added, "With Guillaume's phalange."

"You've already been up?" I asked doubtfully. "You were awake?" Silvan was the original night owl. He strived his hardest not to experience much of the morning.

Silvan yawned. "I made a point of remembering. George isn't the only man with honour, you know?"

I breathed a sigh of relief. "Oh... well... that's great. Thank you. I was worried about him getting into trouble. He did us a huge favour."

"He most certainly did. I must say it was a tad brisk standing on the step waiting for him to turn up. My feet are frozen. Now, if you don't mind? I intend to catch another few hours of shut-eye."

"Of course. Sorry." I stepped backwards into the corridor.

"Unless you want to join me?" Silvan lifted the duvet as an invitation.

"In your dreams," I growled, and slammed the door on his laughter.

Later, when decorum had been restored all around, and my guests were comfortable and fed and off doing the things they wanted to be doing, Gwyn joined Silvan and I as we shared a pot of coffee at the kitchen table.

Monsieur Emietter chopped carrots at a lightening pace, while Florence mixed several cake batters at once, poring over a cookbook she'd found in the attic somewhere with studious concentration.

"I need to apologise to you, Alfhild," Gwyn said, surprising me from the get-go. "I couldn't be entirely honest with you before, but now I see that things have progressed. You ought to hear my side of the story."

"I'd love to hear it," I replied gently. "Do you mind Silvan being here?"

Gwyn examined the dark wizard next to me and shook her head. "No, I think he's in as deep as you are."

That sounded oddly ominous and not what I expected to hear at all. I suppose I'd assumed that now we knew that Guillaume had died of natural causes, I could be slightly less concerned. That didn't really explain why he'd been shut up in a cavity in the wall of course, but it was easier to digest.

"Guillaume was a regular visitor to the inn, right back from when I first married James, your great-grandfather and arrived here in 1919. Occasionally he visited us with his young friend."

"William Wylie?" I asked and Gwyn nodded.

"Yes. William." She paused and her face clouded with momentary sadness. "From the first moment I met Guillaume I recognised him as an extraordinary wizard. We had a great deal in common. He was much older than I and given that my own father had died when I was a young girl, I think I saw in him the father figure I'd been lacking for so long. I very much looked forward to his visits to the inn."

She smiled, casting her mind back through the long years. "I had a vague inkling that Guillaume belonged to some sort of secret order, and I often felt that he went away to do business."

"Why did you think that?" Silvan asked.

Gwyn thought for a moment. "I sensed that he and William had a business relationship of some kind. William deferred to Guillaume in most things, and when they were together at the inn they really were as thick as thieves. When Guillaume came alone, he was more relaxed. We would walk in Speckled Wood, play games on the lawn, play bridge in The Snug. He was excellent company. Full of tall tales and quirky stories."

"Did he ever tell you which order he belonged

to?" How much had my great-grandmother known about him, I wondered.

"At the end," Gwyn replied, her face full of woe.

"What happened," I asked softly, gently nudging her to go on.

"The final time he visited us here he was alone. He was taken ill, suddenly, one evening after supper. James and I helped him to his bedroom to rest. I wanted to get a doctor in, but Guillaume wouldn't hear of it. He kept saying he'd feel much better after a good night's sleep. But something told me he wouldn't. I sat with him, through the night, and his condition deteriorated to the point that it became obvious—even to him—that he was failing." Gwyn paused and rolled her shoulders back.

"Then he swore me to secrecy. 'Alfhild,' he said, 'what I'm about to tell you must remain between the two of us'. And he told me about his highly secret order. Eventually he asked that when he passed over to the next world, that I hide him and all his belongings in a secret place. And bind it with the most powerful magick known, so that nobody could find him."

I cocked my head, puzzled. "He didn't want you to reach out to the order? Or to William Wylie?"

Gwyn looked troubled. "Time was very short,

and looking back, I may have become confused. I was young. I was close to panic. I wanted to honour him by following his instructions to the letter."

"And you knew the magick?" Silvan asked.

Gwyn emitted a tight laugh. "By all that's green, no I did not. But he'd even thought of that." She mimed holding a stick in two hands. "He carried a staff. He gave it to me and told me I could use it to create a powerful forcefield around him." She swallowed. "Just before dawn he stopped breathing. I remember standing at the window, watching the sun coming up on a glorious day, knowing he wouldn't see it. It fair broke my heart, I must admit."

Gwyn's voice cracked and she dropped her head to her chin. We gave her a moment to remember the man she had been so fond of.

"I couldn't do as he'd requested by myself. I had to enlist James for assistance. We didn't really discuss it. He knew I wouldn't have asked him to hide the death unless it had been Guillaume's will. We decided to temporarily hide Guillaume's body in the bedroom next door while we had the partition built. We chose carpenters from Honiton, just far enough away that they had no reason to question why we wanted to make the larger bedroom smaller. Then we stowed Guillaume's body in the corner. I arranged him so that he was sitting upright, with his book in his lap, his hands folded on top of it, because he looked so peaceful that way."

I remembered how he'd been found. "And that's the way he remained until we stumbled across him when we went to add the en suite." No wonder Gwyn had been so against that idea. "Why was he so adamant that he be kept secret? He must have been missed, mustn't he?"

"But that's the beauty of time travel, isn't it?" Silvan pointed out. "He'd been going backwards and forwards in time all his adult life. Maybe he counted on the fact that no-one could ever be sure of where he would be and when."

I thought about what Silvan was saying and my brain exploded. "Is that the way time travel works?"

Silvan widened his eyes and shrugged. He had no idea, either. He was winging it.

Gwyn had fallen silent, I realised. There was something more. Silvan noticed it too, and of course, given that he trod a darker path than I, was quicker to cotton on to it.

"Except..." he said, drawing the word out as he thought aloud. "Maybe it wasn't himself he was trying to hide. Maybe he was hiding something he had in his possession."

By the way that Gwyn's eyes glinted I instinctively knew Silvan had hit upon it. "But what could that have been? I mean... there were a few photos and a book... nothing of any real interest."

Silvan turned to me with excitement. "But think about it. We know the forcefield had been breached. What if someone had managed to do that and take something of value."

"The thing that Guillaume was trying to hide." That made perfect sense. "I wonder what it was."

Florence dropped a spoon with a clatter and startled I glanced up. She was gazing over towards the door behind me, the one that linked to the back passage.

"Where on earth did you come from?" she asked.

Three heads swivelled as one. William Wylie had appeared in the doorway, dressed as always in his smart, slightly dated suit.

"The thing that Guillaume was trying to hide? It was Gorde's Gimcrack," he said. "And I've been trying to find it for over a century."

"Gorde's Grimcrack?" I asked.

"Gimcrack," Mr Wylie repeated, correcting me.

"That was his name, wasn't it? Gorde." This gimcrack had been named after him?

Mr Wylie strode into the room. Monsieur Emietter regarded him with suspicion, as he did all strangers who entered the kitchen while the chef was going about his work.

"It was. Guillaume invented the Gimcrack and it was named after him."

"And what is a gimcrack when it's at home?" I pressed.

"I really can't say, I'm afraid. That's classified information."

"I see." I was disappointed not to be able to find out more.

But Silvan wasn't so easily rebuffed. "I'm going to hazard a guess that it's something to do with time travel. Given Guillaume was a time-travelling wizard and a gimcrack is some sort of thrown-together invention...?"

Mr Wylie bristled at Silvan's words. "Guillaume was a genius. The Gimcrack wasn't exactly thrown together like some shoddy children's kindergarten model concocted from cereal boxes. He took years to perfect it." He walked over to the kitchen table and stared down at us. "He used to laughingly refer to it as his little trinket, but over the years he single-handedly perfected the invention that allows our order to travel anywhere at any time without adverse effects."

Silvan gazed up at Mr Wylie, completely intrigued. "How does it do that?"

Mr Wylie folded his arms. "Like I told you, it's classified."

Silvan sniffed. We were obviously at an impasse.

"And this is the item that was removed from Gorde's body?" I asked. "Assuming it was there in the first place?"

As one we turned to look at Gwyn. She shuffled under our scrutiny. "I... I... I'm not sure. I don't know what it looked like."

Mr Wylie turned to me. "I believe you have my briefcase?"

The blasted briefcase. "I do. It's been difficult to lose. And believe me I did try on several occasions." I turned for the door. "Give me a minute."

I dashed up the back stairs to my office, half expecting the briefcase to have disappeared, but it remained where I'd stowed it, safely under my desk. I picked it up, light as a feather, and ran back down the stairs once more, where the others waited for me, the only sound in the kitchen, Monsieur Emietter's rapid chopping. He'd switched from carrots to celery now.

I placed the briefcase on the kitchen table and stood back as Mr Wylie flipped the clasps. Of course, it looked empty once more, but with just a tiny flick of a finger Mr Wylie unveiled the contents. He rummaged among what was there but couldn't find what he was looking for. A firmer wag of his finger and yet more items appeared, the briefcase brimming with a variety of weird items.

"Double-layered magick." Silvan nodded in approval. "Nice."

The corner of Mr Wylie's mouth tilted up. "Thank you. It takes years to perfect." He held up a gold contraption, about the size of the palm of my hand. It looked something like a large alarm clock, but with the innards on the outside. Coils, springs and cogs had been neatly crafted together around a central glass window around two inches in diameter.

Mr Wylie pressed a button and the small window began to glow sky blue.

"Gorde's Gimcrack," he showed Gwyn. "But this one is mine."

"Wow," Silvan exclaimed, and I smiled in amusement. I could sense his desire to get his hands on it from where I was standing.

Gwyn nodded her confirmation. "Yes. We left a

little machine like this with him. And no, it wasn't there when his body was recovered."

Aghast, I turned to Mr Wylie. "So it was stolen!" I indicated Silvan. "We found that the forcefield had been interfered with."

Worry scored deep lines in Mr Wylie's face. "Could you pinpoint when exactly?"

"No," Silvan replied reluctantly. "There was so little time. I would say thirty to forty years ago, but the magick that repaired the rift made a good job of hiding that detail."

"Probably on purpose. If you're going to steal a time-travelling machine, you don't want fellow time-travellers to come and interrupt you while you're doing it. If that happened, they would have the knowledge after the fact." Mr Wylie steepled his fingers. "I'd been hoping I could target the precise moment the Gimcrack was stolen."

"To go back and prevent it happening?" Silvan nodded his understanding, his face grim.

"Exactly. And that's why I've been attempting to make inroads in tracking it down in all of these years." Mr Wylie squeezed his own Gimcrack and the blue light brightened through the glass.

"Wasn't it rather dangerous leaving your gimcrack in the briefcase?" I asked. "At the airport, at the coach station, at the post office. What if someone else had found it?" I asked.

Mr Wylie looked coy. "But they didn't, did they, Alfhild? You've looked after it extremely well. I couldn't have asked for a better guardian." I couldn't help but feel this was a jibe at Gwyn who hadn't—in the end—been able to keep Gorde's Gimcrack safe. I frowned.

Silvan intervened before I could rebut Mr Wylie. "What do you intend to do now?" he asked.

"I think you'll find that's my business and not yours," Mr Wylie replied politely, snapping the clasps of the briefcase and snatching it up with his left hand. He brandished the Gimcrack in his right, pressed a button again and the light blinked. "Good day to you." With one sharp pale blue flash, he vanished, leaving everyone in the kitchen blinking into the vacuum he'd created.

Silvan raised his eyebrows and sank bank on his seat. "Well, well, well. That was interesting."

"Wasn't it?" I glanced at poor Gwyn, looking more miserable than ever. "Don't worry, Grandmama. You couldn't have known Gorde's Gimcrack would be stolen. This is not your fault. None of it is. Mr Wylie was unfair to insinuate such a thing."

"Agreed," said Silvan.

"Do you think so?" Gwyn asked. "I let my old friend down. There's no getting away from that." She whirled around and apparated out of the kitchen. I stared into the empty space where she'd been and hoped she wouldn't stay away for long this time.

Meanwhile Florence had started to pour cake batter into the baking tins on top of the work surface. For some reason she'd created a blue mix. The colour reminded me of Wylie's Gimcrack.

I took a seat opposite Silvan and met his gaze. His black eyes sparkled as he studied my face. "The little cogs of your mind are whirring noisily, Alfhild. What a student you are. Your suspicion does you credit."

I scowled at him. Trust him to take the credit for my negative thoughts. "Something's not right."

Silvan nodded. "My instinct, too." Behind him, Florence slammed her cake pans into the oven and startled me. Silvan, as always remined icy calm. "There's more to this than meets the eye."

Chapter Thirteen

Later, carrying a mug of hot chocolate and a Sunday newspaper supplement up to my bedroom, I made preparations for a stress-free hour or so, relaxing before attempting to drift off to sleep. Mr Hoo occupied his usual place on my twisted iron bedstead, and I stroked his head before lighting a candle and turning my duvet down.

As I perched on the side of the bed to pull off my shoes and stockings, Mr Hoo began to flap his wings. Given his wingspan of around three feet, you can imagine the amount of breeze he created.

"What's up, fella?" I asked and turned to soothe him, but this seemed to make him worse.

"Are you alright?" I asked in alarm, reaching for him once more, but as I did so, he shot away from me and headed for the window. Whenever Mr Hoo took up residence in the bedroom, I left the window open.

I only ever closed it if he was out hunting and the weather had turned inclement. Now it stood partially ajar, but not wide enough for him to exit gracefully while he was in such a tearing hurry. He thunked against the glass and then fell head first out of the window.

I shrieked and rushed forwards, unlatching the window all the way and leaning out, scared to death of what I would see.

"Mr Hoo? Mr Hoo?" I called in panic. It was difficult to make out much in the darkness, but I thought I could see his little body on the ground beneath my window. "Noooooo!"

I abandoned everything and rushed out of my bedroom. "I'm coming!" I called as I clattered down the stairs, slipping the last few and landing awkwardly on the hard floor of the back corridor. Picking myself up I chased through the bar and then out of the front door. I pelted along the front of the inn and found Mr Hoo perched on the side of an old water trough we used as a planter, watching me.

"You scared me to death!" I scolded. "Are you alright? Let me check you over." I moved closer to my feathered friend and he fluttered away.

"What's the matter?" I asked, genuinely perplexed. "Are you hurt?" I slid forwards and he took to the wing, soaring through the air and onto the lawn, where he landed gracefully and turned to regard me with his orange caramel eyes.

"You're behaving peculiarly." I ventured out onto the lawn towards him. As I drew close, he moved off again, settling about twelve feet away. I paused. Ahead of us lay Speckled Wood. Mr Hoo did not appear to be hurt, or even stunned. He could make it to Speckled Wood by himself if he really wanted to.

A lightbulb went on in my brain. "Do you want me to follow you?" I asked.

"Hooo-oooo. Hooo ooo hoo. Tw'it."

I shook my head at him. "Alright I'm coming. And I'm not a twit."

I didn't have a torch, so I had to navigate through the wood by the light of the moon. Fortunately, it was a clear and dry night and there was enough light for me to remain on the path. Mr Hoo flew from branch to branch ahead of me, sometimes circling back if I fell behind. He could fly much faster than I could stumble over the roots of trees.

The very air in the wood teemed with life

tonight. The marsh had been cleansed by Vance with the natural assistance of some wonderful thunderstorms and cloudbursts during the course of the summer. Speckled Wood itself began fairly high up in the hills above Whittlecombe, and as a result rainwater had flushed through the system easily enough as it ran down the paths and gullies, diluting the toxic nature of the chemicals planted at the source of our freshwater springs. As I walked into the wood, I was delighted to feel the steady pulse of a healthy living beat beneath my palm when I lightly trailed my hand across the front of the trees' trunks.

After a few minutes of half-walking-half-jogging in pursuit of Mr Hoo, I realised he was leading me to the clearing. I slowed down to a more comfortable pace and watched where I was putting my feet. The last thing I wanted was to turn an ankle.

We had almost arrived at our destination when I sensed the presence of another. Not unduly alarmed I reached inside my robes for my wand, freeing it as a precaution. The chances were that Finbarr and his pixies were out and about tonight. He preferred walking the perimeter of my property at night and sleeping during the day.

But Finbarr wasn't why Mr Hoo had led me out here, was he?

I halted, listening intently. From somewhere behind me came a muffled curse.

Silvan.

“Hey?” I called softly and heard the shuffle of feet speeding up slightly as he walked through dead leaves. I peered into the darkness until I could make him out. Silvan’s preference for all-black clothing made him difficult to spot in the dark.

“What are you doing here?” I asked when he drew level with me.

He leaned closer until I could smell the faint scent of whisky, and something else, a slight spice. His eau-de-cologne. Pleasant.

“Following you,” he whispered conspiratorially, and I pushed him away.

“How did you know I’d left the inn?”

Silvan laughed gently. “Everyone in this wretched village knows you left the inn after all that kerfuffle you were making.”

I giggled. “I was in a bit of a panic, admittedly.”

“What happened?”

I pointed up ahead to where Mr Hoo waited on a branch, his bright eyes staring in our direction. “Mr Hoo gave a great dramatic performance, pretending to fall out of the window.”

Silvan snorted.

"Hooo ooo. Hooo ooo," Mr Hoo returned in answer, and we joined him at the edge of the clearing in the centre of the forest.

"So now what?" I asked, turning around slowly and scanning the shadows.

"We wait, I suppose. There must be a reason why Mr Hoo wanted you here." Silvan made himself comfortable on a bench, patting the space beside himself. After a moment I joined him.

We didn't have to wait long. A sudden flash of blue light announced Mr Wylie's return. His greeting, "Good evening," originated in the air above us, and then he stepped of the blackness—seemingly from nowhere—and joined us.

"You brought us here?" I blinked in surprise.

Mr Wylie smiled. "With the help of Mr Hoo."

"Hmm." I regarded my feathered friend with suspicion. Whose side was he on?

"Why all the cloak and daggers, my friend?" Silvan asked. "Not that I mind a little skulduggery, but generally I'm the one at the heart of it, not the one on the outside."

Mr Wylie lifted his right hand. He was still carrying both the Gimcrack and his briefcase. "I apologise for not being clear and upfront about my plans, but I had to be sure we weren't being spied upon." He indicated the clearing. "In discussion with Mr Hoo this seemed the most secure location."

"Is that so?" I asked and Mr Hoo wobbled his head.

"I need your help," Mr Wylie said.

Silvan grunted. "You could just ask for it. I'm sure Alfhild would oblige." I favoured my dark friend with a warning look, but he simply smirked at me. "You love helping people, Alf. Admit it. You're naturally a good Samaritan. You like to get involved in anything and everything."

I couldn't deny I'd had plenty of adventures since arriving at Whittle Inn.

"*And* you're incredibly nosy," Silvan finished.

I decided to ignore him. "How can we help you?" I asked Mr Wylie.

"I'd like you to assist me in my attempts to track down Gorde's Gimcrack."

"Wouldn't we be better off searching for that back at the inn?" I asked and Mr Wylie shook his head.

"No. I'm afraid its long gone from there."

"So—"

"Take my arm, Alfhild, if you wouldn't mind." He held out the arm that was holding the briefcase and I pocketed my wand so that I could reach out to hold him at the elbow with my right hand. "And Silvan, if you could catch a hold of Alfhild?" Silvan grinned, his eyes glinting with mischief as he laced his fingers through mine. I went to wrench my hand from his in annoyance, when suddenly the world lurched to one side and I was glad to be holding on to anything.

I heard Mr Hoo squawk in alarm and then the woods spun around me, slowly at first and then faster and faster, the landscape melting into an amorphous dark mass. My ears popped and my stomach heaved as the floor seemed to drop away and stars exploded around me, and then thankfully there was nothing.

I blinked.

Lights flashed in the corner of my vision, and my stomach churned with motion sickness.

"Here. Here. Take this." Someone was waving something in front of my nose and I weakly batted them away.

"It's okay, Alf." Silvan's voice, gentle, his hand landing on my shoulder. "Take a good sniff of this."

I inhaled. Ginger. Bergamot. Or freshly cut grass.

The spinning began to slow, and Silvan's face, etched with concern, came sharply into focus.

"What—?" I groaned.

"Some form of time travel, I'd guess," Silvan said, patting my arm. "Are you feeling better?"

I clutched at my head. "Whoa. No. I wouldn't want to do that more than once."

Silvan shook his head, a wry smile on his lips. "You're obviously not a natural time traveller. I'm afraid we will have to do it again because we're going to have to get home at some stage." He stood and moved away from me, but I struggled to follow him with my eyes, my vision seemed to be fading in and out of focus.

Then a vision in saffron appeared in front of me, holding out a beaker of steaming liquid. "Drink this. It will help to settle your stomach and clear your mind."

I looked up. "Mr Wylie?"

"The very same." He had removed his suit and donned robes, the same as those we'd seen on Guillaume's body when we'd found him, except these were new. Clean. Crisp. The multi-colours at the hem bright and sparkling. "Welcome to my home."

I looked around, curious as to where someone like Mr Wylie would live. We appeared to be inside a large glass igloo. Above our heads a zillion stars sparkled in a deep, denim blue sky. They snatched my breath away with their sheer impossible infiniteness.

"That's quite a view," I said, catching a sense of the shaky wonder of it in my own voice.

Mr Wylie laughed. "Drink."

I took a couple of sips of the liquid in the beaker. Again, the taste of ginger with lemon and something else. He was right. My head began to defuzz and the churning sensation in my stomach calmed down. Eventually when I figured I could walk without falling over, I pushed myself to standing.

"Where are we?" Silvan was asking, and I followed the sound of his voice to join them in a different part of the structure. It reminded me in part of some science-fiction dome, forged from hexagonal shapes. A kind of 'my-great-grandmother's-new-greenhouse-meets-an-oversized-beehive' thingie.

The larger dome housed a laboratory of some description, replete with refrigerator sized computers, giant floating TV display screens and more-oddly, an old-fashioned carpenter's workbench. Boxes of metal scraps were scattered around the place, and tools of every size littered each worksurface.

"I'm afraid I can't share much information with you. This is all highly secret. I've had to obtain explicit permission to bring you here. You can't ever talk about this with anyone else. I hope you understand."

"Of course," I reassured Mr Wylie and he looked relieved.

"What I can tell you is these are my quarters. All the wizards in my order have a similar space. Novices share accommodation."

This smaller dome was therefore Mr Wylie's personal space. It contained little more than a bed and a squishy sofa. That was it.

Now I moved from the smaller dome to the larger one to join Silvan and Mr Wylie, and—to my surprise—Mr Hoo.

"What's he doing here?" I asked in alarm. The last thing I wanted was my owl loose in space somewhere.

Wait. Am I in space? Do I want to be in space?

The thought had my head spinning once more, and for once I didn't push Silvan away when he came over to take my arm. "Here. You can sit on this chair," he said, and I gratefully sank onto a hard-wood chair with a curved back and bowl. I supped at my ginger drink some more, my hands trembling slightly.

"I think Mr Hoo fancied a change of scene," Silvan said.

"Hooo ooo," Mr Hoo called in evident satisfaction.

"Don't worry about this little fellow. He'll be fine," Mr Wylie chipped in.

I groaned. "Why isn't anyone else as sick as me?"

"It's unfortunate, but the jump through time and space does upset some people more than others." Mr Wylie commiserated.

Silvan however, merely tittered. "You're obviously a delicate flower, Alfhild. More at home in the forest than in space."

I glared at him. How could he feel so at ease here? So naturally at home everywhere? It irked me that he could be so adaptable, so flexible, permanently in his comfort zone. The man was impossible.

"This is my planodome," Mr Wylie continued. "As I've said, unfortunately I really can't offer you much in the way of detail. This is all confidential. But I was granted special dispensation to bring you here so that you could help me." He smiled down at me. "When Alfhild is feeling better I'm going to take you to the maxidome which is a kind of central hub.

You'll have the opportunity to meet some other members of my order."

"I'm fine." I drained my drink. "I feel much better."

"If you're sure?" Mr Wylie regarded me doubtfully.

"Lead on." I smiled to show him how wonderfully well I'd recuperated.

"This way, then." Mr Wylie took a few steps forwards and clicked his fingers. The floor parted, exposing a well-lit staircase heading down to a pristine area below.

"Excellent," Silvan exclaimed, his face gleeful like a small boy at Christmas. I fell in step behind him.

"Hoo woo. Hooo-ooo."

"You can pipe down," I told my owl. "You got me into this mess in the first place."

The maxidome was reached via the staircase and an extremely long tunnel. It reminded me in part of the London Underground—a similar sort of arched shape to the walls, and lots of white tiling. But this was spotlessly clean and there were no posters on the walls. In fact, there was very little to break up the monotony of all the shiny white surfaces, apart from other staircases, also tiled in white, and the odd silver door in the ceiling.

Given the length of the tunnel and the distance we needed to cover, as well as the shifting unease of my stomach—how I now regretted the extra-large slice of Florence's blueberry cake I'd polished off after dinner—I was pleased to see a small open-topped buggy waiting for us at the foot of Mr Wylie's staircase. We climbed inside, Mr Hoo perching on the safety railing. The driverless vehicle took off at a relatively sedate 20 mph.

Silvan kept the secretive Mr Wylie in conversation, quizzing him about the planodome and such things, but I don't think he made much headway. In any case, I zoned them out, speculating about what exactly Mr Wylie had in mind for us.

The buggy came to a stop outside a pair of double doors. Unlike the rest of the doors I'd spied in the tunnel these were black, so there could be no mistaking them. Little cameras spied down on us from the ceiling, and Mr Wylie waved. Eventually the doors opened, and the buggy was able to pass through. I lifted my arm so that Mr Hoo could settle on the back of my wrist and then we disembarked.

We found ourselves in the most enormous glass structure I have ever seen.

We'd been under the impression that the Cosmic Order of Chronometric Wizards consisted of a dozen or so time travelling souls. At first glance it seemed we couldn't have been more wrong.

Everywhere I looked there were groups of saffron-clad robe-wearing men and women working industriously at small shining stations. They gazed up at screens or pointed at maps. They donned goggles and produced tiny explosions of light. As we walked past the first of these stations, I could see that the enormous map here was actually a constellation. The wizards were talking, with a great deal of gesticulation and passion, about stars and a route through them.

Mr Wylie followed my gaze as we walked past them, my head swivelling to keep watching them even once we'd passed.

"They're students," he explained. "They're learning the best way to move through a particular galaxy. We wouldn't want to scramble our signals by travelling through an unexpected asteroid belt, now, would we?"

I grimaced, liking the idea of time-travel less and less. "No, I don't suppose you would."

The deeper into the dome we ventured, the more incredible everything appeared. We walked through an area dedicated to workbenches. Wizards were busily employed, some with mallets and hammers, other with delicate surgical implements. There were tools displayed on floating boards that gracefully weaved in and out of those working here—containing implements of every conceivable shape and size and in every possible metal. For the most part, the wizards here had their heads bent over tiny hand sized machines that looked very similar to Gorde's Gimcrack.

There were conveyor belts rolling along on tank tracks containing cogs and spokes, springs and clips. Wizards would dash across and inspect the wares on offer and then pluck one or two pieces, perhaps discard one, and then race back to the workbench to add it to their creation.

Dotted here and there were wizards in darker orange robes but with similar decoration. They pushed brooms around, sweeping up pins and screws and shavings of metal from the glimmering floor. There didn't appear to be a speck of dust anywhere. Florence would approve.

"Does every wizard create their own Gimcrack?" Silvan asked, and I stared at him in surprise. He'd hit the nail on the head. Of course, that's what these men and women around us were doing.

Mr Wylie nodded. "Well spotted. Any wizard worth his or her salt is going to be able to get their head around the complexity of the Gimcrack." Mr Wylie halted at a bench to our right so that Silvan could get a better look at what the wizards were building here. The creation seemed similar to Gorde's Gimcrack, but it lacked the refinement, the meticulous placing of the components that made Guillaume's so intricate and specialised.

Even I could see that.

But that in itself raised an interesting question in my mind.

"Gorde wasn't the first to make one?" I asked. It stood to reason that Guillaume wasn't the first time-travelling wizard. How had these wizards moved around before he invented the Gimcrack?

"Gorde's Gimcrack is *the* archetype. It has yet to be improved upon," came Mr Wylie's curt response. But it didn't answer my question. I looked across at Silvan to see whether he had noticed the avoidance of my question and he smiled devilishly at me, but also gave the tiniest of headshakes.

A frisson of relief flowed through me. I'd felt uneasy since our earlier encounter with Mr Wylie, but if Silvan was playing it cool, I had nothing to worry about. After all, he was no fool.

Mr Wylie led us through increasingly sterile areas until at least we came across a screened-off space. An older woman, in the usual saffron robes regarded us with interest as we approached. "These are our guests?" she asked, and Mr Wylie nodded.

"Come through, come through," she sang, and the screens pulled back to reveal what I can only describe as a stage set, within the bigger dome. Taking the shape of an ordinary domestic room it was as far from being sparsely furnished as it was possible to be. It remined me in part of Wizard Shadowmender's peculiar house in Surbiton. Setting foot in here, with no knowledge of what was going on in the immediate vicinity behind you, you might actually have imagined yourself inside a brick constructed dwelling. The walls suggested such. They were oak panelled at the bottom, and then covered in a dark wine brocade above a line of beading that continued all the way around the ceiling. It made for an odd effect, inducing slight claustrophobia. Peculiarly, there was a dentist's chair in the middle of the chequered floor. It had been hooked up to numerous screens and a large computer. The only other items of furniture were an old desk and a pair of scruffy wooden chairs.

Most striking of all were the sheer number of clocks in the room. Some were free standing—tall Grandfather and smaller Grandmother clocks, others—Swiss cuckoo clocks and their ilk—had been hung on hooks. Still more, many dozens more, had been arranged on shelves.

I gaped in astonishment. The clocks ticked and tocked, clicked and whirred, and I was reminded of the clock shop in Celestial Street.

Footsteps behind us alerted me to a pair of newcomers. Two young wizards, physically strong if not magickly so. The screens swished closed behind them. One of them nodded at me, the other looked only forwards. Guards?

Why did we need guards? Instantly I was on high alert.

The woman cleared her throat gently, diverting my attention.

"Pardon me for not coming to meet you sooner. Unfortunately, we are experiencing a number of issues with the main timeframe software. I am Acting High Wizard Ballulah Borodov, and I am honoured to make your acquaintance." She bowed slightly and smiled at first Silvan and then me. "Mr Wylie has been acting under my instructions. As you are probably already aware, we have been trying to track down the whereabouts of Guillaume Gorde for many decades. In fact, as we stand here in this instance of time, we have been searching for centuries."

Centuries? We'd jumped forwards in time? No wonder my stomach was having a hard time coping.

"We've had no luck. Ms Daemonne?" Ballulah scanned my face. "Your great-grandmother, with the aid of Gorde's magic staff, was able to create a monumentally powerful forcefield. That in itself would have kept him hidden forever, or at least until Whittle Inn was razed to the ground."

I eyed the Acting High Wizard thoughtfully. I didn't like the way she'd said that.

"Hoooo." Mr Hoo, still on my wrist, ruffled his feathers. I soothed him with my free hand. He obviously sensed some ulterior intent behind the Acting High Wizard's words, too.

"In-and-of-itself that powerful magick was no bad thing. The problem only came about when the forcefield was breached and Gorde's Gimcrack was stolen," Ballulah continued, "and that is our property which we have no alternative but to retrieve."

She regarded us solemnly. "Given that your great-grandmother is now deceased and cannot aid us further with our enquiries, we need your assistance."

"I'm sure we're happy to try and help you," I nodded at Ballulah, wondering what form our help could take. A scratching feeling on the top of my scalp had me feeling uncomfortable.

Ballulah smiled, and this time there was a hint of steel in her eye. "I'm afraid there is no try. To put it plainly, we must succeed. The fate of our Order hangs in the balance."

Silvan shifted his weight slightly beside me, a hint that his defences were up. "For the sake of Gorde's Gimcrack? Surely if all wizards make their own gimcrack then—"

Ballulah raised her hands. "There is no more discussion to be had." She nodded at the wizard guards behind me and quick as a flash one of them had hold of me by the upper arms, and the other had pulled a hessian sack over Mr Hoo.

Silvan reached for his wand but Ballulah reached out an arm and stopped him. "I do apologise,

Mr Silvanus. I had your wands confiscated when you both arrived."

I glared at William Wylie. What mess had he mired us in? He had the grace to drop my gaze and look a little shamefaced.

"Mr Silvanus, if you wouldn't mind taking a seat, here?" Ballulah indicated the chair I'd likened to a dentist's chair. I suppose it was actually more of a reclining leather couch in blue leather.

Silvan's gaze raked over first me and then the wizard who held me in an iron grip, and finally the sack containing a fluttering and flustered and hissing Mr Hoo. "You know, there's really no need for this," he snarled at Ballulah. "We're happy to assist you, but this—"

"Please take a seat," Ballulah repeated smoothly. Silvan's ire did not bother her in the slightest. When he didn't move, the smile on her face disappeared. "Nobody will come to harm here. Your cooperation is appreciated. Now please," Ballulah indicated the seat once more and reluctantly Silvan climbed onto it.

With practised ease, Ballulah slipped manacles around Silvan's wrists, effectively strapping him to the chair.

"What are you doing?" I cried and wrenched

free of the goon holding me. "We said we would help you if we could. This is coercive!" The wizard guard made to grab me again, so I kicked him hard in the groin. He doubled over with a shriek. I gave him another for good measure.

"Ms Daemonne—" Ballulah called.

I swivelled on the balls of my feet and directed a short sharp punch of magick—effectively a hard slap on the cheek—at the guard holding my owl in his hessian sack. Ballulah sent a blocking spell his way to stop me making contact with him but she wasn't fast enough. He dropped the sack and I quickly extracted an indignant Mr Hoo, who fluttered to the top of a Grandfather clock and began grooming his feathers with a hitherto unseen fury.

I turned back to Ballulah. "Ms Daemonne—" she warned.

"This is just not civilised," I said and lifted my hands to cast a spell her way. So what if she'd taken our wands? Any witch who knows her onions can easily use her hands. I'd knock her on her backside if she insisted in carrying on with this charade.

Instead she threw back her head and laughed in delight and began to applaud. Mr Wylie smirked, too. At the same time, a screen, previously invisible to the naked eye flew down from the ceiling and floated in the air in front of us. It blinked on and Wizard Shadowmender's face smiled down at me.

"Hello, Alf," he boomed at me.

"Wizard Shadowmender?" I glanced around in confusion. The guard on the floor, his eyes watering, was being helped to his feet by the other one. "What's going on here?"

"I do apologise for all the subterfuge, my dear. I have been trying to convince Acting High Wizard Borodov that it wasn't necessary, but she feared you might be a little meek and mild for what she intends to ask of you."

Ballulah laughed again and pointed at the guard I'd wiped out. "I happily admit to being wrong. This pair have plenty of backbone." She nodded at Mr Hoo's tormentor, "Miguel, please release Mr Silvanus."

As he moved to do so, I peered up at Wizard Shadowmender. "I was worried there for a minute."

"Alf, as you've correctly surmised, there is more to Gorde's Gimcrack than meets the eye. If I might have a word with your... friend?"

Silvan came and stood beside me, cocking an eyebrow my way in amusement.

"You remember Wizard Shadowmender?" I asked him, pointing at the screen. He nodded at me, so I mouthed the words 'be nice' at him so that no-one else would overhear.

"I do." Silvan turned to the screen. "Good to see you again, Sir."

"Likewise, young Horace," Shadowmender beamed down at us. "Horace, if it is at all possible, Ballulah would like to harvest some of your memories."

"Which ones specifically?" Silvan looked a little worried, and not without cause. I could understand that. As a rogue and a scoundrel, it stood to reason Silvan's memories were a cesspit of shadiness.

"We understand you performed a little necromancy the other night?" Shadowmender trod carefully. It was not something our order particularly approved of.

Silvan glanced sideways at me and I shrugged. I'd mentioned to him before that there were never any secrets at Whittle Inn.

"I did," Silvan's voice was clear and calm, without the faintest hint of guilt. I'd never known him to be phased by any situation. I certainly admired him for that. "I really wasn't able to find much out."

Ballulah shuffled forwards once more, her whole appearance had changed from the haughty Acting

High Wizard we'd met before to a friendlier more open and earnest version. "Our advanced technology can replay your memories to look at what happened that night. We'll be able to re-examine the electrical trace energy that you found, and with any luck we can pinpoint a more precise moment that Gorde's Gimcrack was removed from the room and find out who removed it."

"Perhaps even prevent it happening," Mr Wylie chipped in.

"Do you use that machine?" I asked, indicating the dentist's chair.

"Yes, but I can assure you it doesn't hurt at all." Mr Wylie patted the chair and looked expectantly at Silvan.

Silvan looked from me to Ballulah and then up at Wizard Shadowmender. Shadowmender nodded. Silvan turned to me and winked.

"Are you sure?" I asked, but Silvan only made his way over to the recliner and settled back into it.

"Let's do it."

This time there were no straps, clips or buckles. Mr Wylie operated the mechanism that lowered the chair, and then gently hooked Silvan up to the machine using wireless probes that looked like globules of gel. As soon as one of the transparent pods had been placed on Silvan's forehead, the computer screen behind him began to flash and beep.

I shifted forwards to stand a little closer to my inert friend, as Ballulah waved at the ceiling and the lights dimmed.

"I just need you to relax, Silvan," Mr Wylie instructed, his voice low. "Close your eyes if you like. It helps to free you from other distractions." Silvan grinned at me, and then shut his eyes as directed.

Mr Wylie fiddled with the keyboard of his computer and the screen began taking measurements of Silvan's thoughts. The readings reminded me in part of Perdita Pugh's electro-endoquaero, seemingly random and indecipherable unless you knew what you were looking for.

"Could you cast your mind back to the night you performed the ritual. You entered the bedroom at Whittle Inn and made your preparations..." The lights and squiggles on the screen altered, patterns emerging as Silvan remembered. "And then you located the forcefield." The machine blipped and bleeped, orange and green lines shooting across the screen.

"Did you manage to make contact with Guillaume Gorde?" Mr Wylie asked.

Silvan scratched at the skin on his forehead, near

the site of the pod. "I did. Ever so briefly. There was a tear in the fabric of the forcefield and I was able to put my hand through."

"Good! Good!" Ballulah exclaimed. "Focus on that moment."

"Yes, Silvan. If you could remember the moment when you reached through the rip in the forcefield..." Mr Wylie stared at the screen, as orange and blue and green lines zipped and zig-zagged. "And again," said Mr Wylie, his voice still calm, almost soothing. The patterns repeated themselves over and over again until the machine gave one long high-pitched beep and a tiny printer began to spew out paper no bigger than a till receipt.

"Ah here we are," Mr Wylie said, a little more excitement to his tone now. He ripped the first reading off, peered at it and nodded in satisfaction, before taking the next one that came out of the machine and passing it to Ballulah.

She pulled a pair of spectacles out of a pocket in her robes and examined the print in front of her. "Perfect," she announced. "How do you all fancy a trip back to 1983?"

CHAPTER FOURTEEN

The tinny sound of a radio playing drifted across the early evening's airwaves. Elton John's *I'm Still Standing* had morphed into Paul Young's *Wherever I lay My Hat* (*That's my Home*) which seemed somehow appropriate given the current circumstances.

Silvan, Mr Wylie and I stood on the drive outside Whittle Inn gazing up at it. The weather was pleasant for late May 1983. This time my stomach had held it together and I'd made the jump through time without too much nausea.

I cocked my head, appraising the evidence in front of me, trying to remember the first time I'd set eyes on my wonky inn, attempting to measure the changes between 1983 and the present. The 1983 inn looked run down, the once white paint of the cladding had become grimy over the years, streaked with green, the windows filthy. At some stage in the intervening years since then the inn had been repainted. It hadn't even looked this bad when I'd taken over, and I'd had it redone myself since then.

The grounds were untidy, but managed. To the left and to the rear of the inn, Speckled Wood stretched away into the distance. That much hadn't changed. Mr Hoo, who had travelled with us of course, leapt from my wrist and flew off that way to take a look.

Mr Wylie led the way to the front steps of the inn and my apprehension grew. I couldn't quite imagine seeing a younger version of my father here, or my paternal grandparents, either. Fortunately, if memory served me correctly, my father Erik Daemonne had been away at University, so there was little chance I'd meet him.

From the research that the chronometric wizards had undertaken, it seemed evident that the inn had been falling into disrepair for some time. Guests had been few and far between in the early to mid-eighties, and despite the clement weather there wasn't a soul to be seen anywhere in the grounds.

We let ourselves in. The main bar was much as I'd originally found it. Partitioned walls in the place where the huge open fireplace now stood. Hard-board covered the rear of the bar, protecting the mirrors. Cheap wooden tables covered in mismatched veneer, and a revolting carpet that had probably been in situ since the mid-seventies completed the scene. The smell of spilt beer and cigarettes was everywhere, along with the oddly jarring undercurrents of boiled cabbage and furniture polish.

I burned with curiosity, desperate to explore the rest of the inn, but Ballulah had been firm on that score, insisting that we had a job to do and should not be side-tracked.

And so, one after another, we climbed single file up the main staircase to the first floor. The walls were scratched and stained, and only a few cheap flower prints decorated the space. The carpet was an odd shade of mustard with brown swirls, thick enough to muffle the sounds of our footsteps.

We paused several doors down from *The Throne Room*.

We'd discussed this at length before travelling back to this time. We wanted to get close enough to know that the person we needed was here, and then we intended to make the much shorter jump forward in time to the moment he or she broke through the forcefield. At that stage we'd surprise him and wrestle the Gimcrack away from him, perhaps apprehend him to either Ballulah or Wizard Shadowmender's custody.

Silvan had been against this suggestion. Not surprising really, I suppose. There's honour among thieves after all, and Silvan was the king of ne'er-do-wells. However, Ballulah had been adamant. A crime had been committed against the property of the Cosmic Order of Chronometric Wizards and she —rightly or wrongly—wanted to see justice.

She'd returned our wands to us, and we were under strict instructions to immobilise the culprit enough that Mr Wylie would be able to transport him to a place of security that would be agreed upon once he was in our custody.

I could sense Silvan's displeasure at this whole set-up, and I understood his feelings on the matter. Guillaume had died of natural causes and so there was nobody to blame for his death. An opportunistic thief had made the most of a situation he had uncovered. As far as we knew, that was all there was to it.

Ballulah and the other wizards in the Cosmic Order of Chronometric Wizards obviously felt differently. Although I suspected there was more to the story than they were telling us, the facts as they stood, suggested that the only thing missing was

Gorde's Gimcrack, and there was no evidence that it had been put to nefarious purposes in the intervening years since 1983.

I would have liked to discuss this privately with Silvan, but he and I had enjoyed no time to confer as we hadn't been left alone at any stage. For now, we had to go along with Ballulah's plan. Mr Wylie for his part seemed intent on following it to the letter.

For the first time I became aware that someone else, presumably the person listening to the radio downstairs, was in residence. Footsteps were following us up the stairs. There was no time to lose. We had to make ourselves scarce. Holding my finger to my lips, I turned the handle of the door nearest us, praying that it hadn't been locked and that the room beyond was vacant.

One after the other we slipped inside, I quickly closed the door as quietly as I could and pressed myself against it. Outside, the footsteps were muted by the carpet but I heard a woman humming to herself as she passed by. Each of us held our breath. We waited. She continued on her way and a few long moments later we heard the opening and closing of a door down the hall, possibly the office, it came from that direction.

I let out a nervous breath and smiled. "Now

what?" I whispered, turning around to properly survey our location. This was a small room, with woodchip wallpaper painted in terracotta. Someone had come up with the bright idea of sticking a frieze —in lime green, terracotta and yellow—all around the room at the place where the walls met the ceiling. I imagined that the same person considered that the polycotton sheets on the bed, in a less than fetching shade of orange, would pull the overall colour scheme together.

Needless to say, it didn't.

Silvan beckoned us over to the wall. "There's someone next door," he mouthed, and we each lay an ear against the wall and eavesdropped. I could clearly hear someone moving around next door, it sounded like they were knocking on wood.

"Which room are we in?" Silvan asked.

"In my time this would be *Stillwater*, my Dean R Koontz room, so yes, that's *The Throne Room* right next door, the one where Guillaume stayed. He was interred in the space between that and the next room on." *Was still interred,* I thought. We were back in 1983 after all.

Mr Wylie backed away from the wall and studied his Gimcrack. "Then this must be the person we're after." He held his palm-sized machine up, the blue light shining brightly. "Are we ready?"

"No time like the present," Silvan smiled.

"Wands equipped," Mr Wylie instructed, and I pulled mine from my robes.

Mr Wylie held his arms out. Silvan and I grabbed one apiece. Me on the left, Silvan to Mr Wylie's right.

"Wait!" I remembered, "What about Mr Hoo?" But it was too late, and once more I found myself flung through the air like a ragdoll.

Given that the physical distance between where we were in *Stillwater* and where we needed to be in *The Throne Room* only amounted to a matter of metres, you'd imagine that our time-travel jump would have been over in the blink of an eye.

Not so.

In addition, we only needed to jump forwards in time by around fifty-three minutes—according to the readings taken from Silvan's harvested memories in any case—and yet travelling through time took longer than you'd anticipate. Once more I became aware of the stars, and now that my body didn't want to react so negatively to the forces spinning me about, I could spend a little time wondering at the infiniteness of time and space and what a small speck of dust I was in the grand scheme of things… before, pow!

We were in *The Throne Room.*

For a fraction of a moment we were all frozen in time, Mr Wylie, Silvan and I, wands pointing forwards towards a small youngish man. Aged about thirty, he wore casual clothes, a pair of brown corduroy trousers and a khaki coloured jumper with a red V-neck, covered by loose grey robes. Bizarrely, I recognised him, and although that awareness was only vague, it stopped me from acting quickly while my brain tried to process who he was, whether we were friends, or whether he posed any danger to me.

He had created a remarkably neat hole in the wall, square in shape, about a foot and a half high, and a foot off the floor. We caught him as he leaned into the hole. I could barely make out the colours of the forcefield, they weaved weakly in and out of each other—orange, green and blue—obviously damaged by this man. He reared back in shock as we unexpectedly appeared in front of him, a look of astonishment on his face. Faster to react than us, he lifted his wand.

I was slow to respond, and Silvan didn't react at

all. That left Mr Wylie, but he was hampered somewhat given that Silvan had for some reason maintained a firm hold of the cosmic wizard's wand arm. As Mr Wylie endeavoured to take aim at the grey-clad wizard in front of us, his spell was knocked off course. It smashed into the wall to the side of the hole.

That was all the time our quick-witted thief needed. He raised his own wand and with a bright flash disappeared from the room.

Mr Wylie cried out and pulled himself away from Silvan and I, heading for the hole in the wall. I followed and glanced inside. I could clearly see Guillaume's robes and his hands folded in his lap. He looked peaceful, much as he would do when we found him in the future.

Whomever it had been that we'd disturbed in the act, he had what he'd come for. The Gimcrack had gone.

"No!" Mr Wylie shrieked in frustration and I cast a quick glance Silvan's way. His face remained impassive.

"I'm sorry." I said, unsure what had gone wrong. I knew somewhere along the line both Silvan and I had failed. "Maybe we could try it again? Time travel to the same point?"

"We can't come back to exactly the same moment of time ever again," Mr Wylie said. "This isn't *Groundhog Day*."

"That's one of my favourite movies!" I exclaimed. Silvan raised his eyebrows in disbelief. Now was probably not the time to be discussing our top-rated movies.

We were in a predicament. "What about landing a few seconds before instead?" I suggested.

"Can't we find out where he's gone?" Silvan asked, changing the subject, and made his way forwards to the hole in the wall, picking his way among the debris on the floor.

Wylie followed and waved his own Gimcrack around trying to record a trace of the wizard who'd disappeared. "There's nothing here. No trace."

Silvan frowned. "That's a terrible shame. Back to the drawing board?" He sounded genuinely sorry, but I knew him too well. What was he up to?

"I need to get back," Mr Wylie said. "The researchers will need to plot some new time co-ordinates and maybe I can have another go." He pointed at the hole, "But we can't leave Gorde exposed that way."

"Leave it to me," Silvan said, and without further ado, he leaned forward into the hole and with the tip of his wand began to repair the rift in the forcefield by waving it in tiny strokes across the width of the tear. Darning magick. I watched in amazement.

When he had finished, he stood back and admired his handywork. "It's not perfect by any means, but it will hold for now." He winked at me. "Until Alf's builders find it again in a few decades."

Mr Wylie flicked his own wand, and the plaster and wattle and daub that had been littered around the hole jumped back on to the wall and began patching itself up. Again, it wasn't the neatest job, but to the casual observer it would just look like a wall in need of repainting.

"How about if we push this dressing table against the wall?" I suggested, and between the three of us, we shifted the furniture around.

From down the hall came the sound of the office door opening. "Time to go," Mr Wylie said.

"But Mr Hoo!" I called urgently. To no avail. Once more as we gripped Mr Wylie's arm, Whittle Inn disappeared from view and 1983 faded into the mists of time once more.

Silvan and I lay on our backs in the dirt of the clearing. Above us the stars twinkled down, the moonlight filtered through the branches of the trees that surrounded us. We were taking a moment to catch our breath.

"I couldn't be doing all that leaping through time and space every five minutes," I groaned. My stomach heaved once more. Fortunately, it had now been over twelve hours in real time since I'd eaten, and centuries in warped cosmic Time-Lord time-travelly kind of time.

"I don't think the Cosmic Order of Chronometric Wizards will be in a rush to recruit either of us in the immediate future," Silvan replied drolly.

I breathed deeply, filling my lungs with the fresh air I loved so much in my wood. "No, they won't. That's true." I turned my head to look at him in profile. "What did we do?" I asked.

Silvan rolled over and grinned. "I think it's called sabotage."

Chapter Fifteen

Sabotage?

Why did we do that though? And instinctively? Without discussing it. Neither of us had taken the action that had been planned, and we'd let a thief go free. No doubt the Cosmic Order of Chronometric Wizards were going to be far from happy with us.

Mr Wylie already was.

I tossed and turned all night, scared to death that I would never clap eyes on Mr Hoo again. Was he really lost in 1983? Would Mr Wylie have the decency to return him to me? How was I even going to get in touch with the Chronometric Wizards? I would need to appeal to Wizard Shadowmender.

By five a.m. I couldn't stay in bed anymore. There seemed to be no point. The alarm would be going off soon enough anyway. I had a shower and washed my hair, and then made my miserable way down to the kitchen where Florence was preparing breakfast pastries for our continental guests.

I snuck a couple of warm croissants from the side when she wasn't looking, stole the honey from the pantry, and flung myself down on a bench at the big kitchen table. My eyes were grimy from lack of sleep, and while the shower had woken me up to a certain extent, I could tell it was going to be a long day.

Florence gave me the once over and poured a large mug of tea. "You look like you need it, Miss Alf."

I sighed. "I do. I really do."

"What's happened?" my housekeeper asked with just the right amount of alarm.

I tore a chunk of croissant and stuffed it in my gob. "You wouldn't believe me if I told you." My reply was almost inaudible, and Florence shook her head.

"I would. I'm over a hundred years old. Anything is possible."

"I've left my owl in 1983," I cried.

"1983?"

"Yes."

Florence turned back to her pastries. "Really,

Miss Alf, you do tell some right porky pies sometimes."

Her disbelief made me grin for some reason. In my wonky world, anything was possible, until it wasn't. Time travel for some reason was a step too far for Florence, but then, she was a ghost and infinity stretched out in front of her and not behind her.

Otherwise Guillaume Gorde might have been able to come back and help us out.

I paused over my breakfast, honey dripping down my fingers and onto the plate in front of me. Guillaume had obviously been happy to let go and travel to the next world. He hadn't hung around. He hadn't wanted to haunt the inn. He had entrusted my poor great-grandmother with the safekeeping of his worldly goods and physical remains. She had tried to keep her promise.

Then someone had come along and been able to sense the existence of Gorde's Gimcrack even through a powerfully built magickal forcefield. We'd seen who that person was the previous evening, but we didn't know why he'd taken the Gimcrack.

But he wasn't a petty thief, was he? No common or garden witch or wizard. He'd been somebody who had found something that they wanted.

Somebody I had seen before, recently. In the

present day. And now that I thought about it, he must have known me when we locked eyes ...

We had locked eyes.

Suddenly I knew where I'd seen him before. "Suffering salted caramel!" I shrieked, and Florence whirled around in alarm.

"Miss?"

I jumped to my feet, my tea sloshing all over my plate, soaking my croissants.

"I need to go and wake Silvan up." He was going to be thrilled. It wasn't even six o'clock yet. "Be a darling and make us some packed lunch please, Florence. I've a feeling we're going to need some sustenance."

And with that I was spinning on my heel and heading for the top floor.

It looked like I was travelling to London once again.

"You know, I'm not especially welcome around here?" Silvan shifted uneasily. For the first time ever, I'd placed him in a situation that he wasn't comfortable with. In fact, I'd never seen him look quite so uncomfortable. He had been more at home fighting

The Mori in his night shirt than walking along the cobbles here in the narrow street between the warm cosy shops.

"Relax. Surely no-one can take issue with you walking up Celestial Street in the daylight and minding your own business. It's not like you've come here to steal..." I stopped dead in my tracks. "Wait, you haven't ever undertaken any nefarious activities along here, have you?"

"I can't answer that question on the grounds that I might incriminate myself."

I shook my head. "I don't believe you sometimes. We're all one kind. All witches and wizards together, aren't we?"

"Tell that to The Mori," Silvan muttered, and turned to walk back the way we'd come.

I grabbed a hold of his sleeve. "Don't go."

He paused, looking back at me, something knowing in his eyes. "Why? You can handle this by yourself, I'm sure."

"I have no idea what's going to happen when I go in there. I know you don't owe me anything." I certainly had no intention of giving him any more money. "But..." I shrugged.

"But?" Silvan leaned in to me, his face close to mine, holding my gaze.

Crikey, the man could be so infuriating. What did he want? My first born?

I pulled away slightly, oddly disconcerted, his proximity to me making me warm.

"It's up to you. You know?" I replied airily.

"Oh." He bit back a grin. "Well, in that case I'll be off then. Seeing as I'm back here, I might as well head home and find out what Marissa is up to."

His attractive friend. The green-eyed monster kicked me in the stomach. "Whatever," I snapped back.

Silvan nodded. "Good seeing you again, Alfhild. Pop in for afternoon tea the next time you're up here in The Smoke."

I watched him in disbelief as he strolled away. "It'll be lovely to see you," he called back over his shoulder.

I growled at his retreating figure. *Fine. Just fine and dandy.*

Feeling a little disconsolate, I walked a few steps along the street in the direction of *The Half Moon Inn.* I supposed I could nip in and see whether Wizard Shadowmender or anyone else I knew was enjoying a leisurely lunch in there.

But that wasn't how I'd envisaged what would happen today. I wanted to confront the person I thought I'd recognised in *The Throne Room* in 1983, in the here and now.

But maybe I should just abandon my plan altogether. Perhaps there was an element of risk I hadn't considered.

But what of Mr Hoo?

I spun about, ready to chase after Silvan and beg him to help me. Instead I collided with someone loitering directly behind me. I squeaked in alarm. "I'm so sorry! I do beg your pardon!" I pushed myself away, one hand on the man's chest.

Silvan.

He'd come back.

Our eyes locked. A moment of understanding passed between us, something I would deny afterwards. "Well?" he asked.

I shivered. "I want..." I started to say. No. "I *need* you to help me. I'd *like* you to be with me."

Silvan offered me his dastardliest smile. "Well alrighty then. Let's go."

Located next door to my solicitor Penelope Quigwell's office at 14b Celestial Street, number 14 was a clock shop named *Once Upon a Time*. It had inhabited this space for decades. I'd paused outside the window many times, whiling away the minutes if I'd turned up early for Penelope's appointments.

Once Upon a Time was a large old-fashioned store. The wooden façade had been painted a classy dark green, and the lettering on the shop sign above the window had been picked out in green and red. A large gold clock face had been faintly embossed on the window. Peering inside you were struck by the sheer number of items the shop stocked. There were clocks and watches and timepieces of every size, shape, colour, make, brand, material and distinction.

And most of them were ticking away merrily to themselves. I recalled the cacophony of noise during the one occasion I'd entered the shop, especially when the clocks had struck the hour while I'd been hiding. According to the clocks on display the time now was just after one. That was a blessed relief.

A slight movement towards the back alerted us to the presence of the proprietor at the rear of the shop. We peered through the glass.

I recalled the day, over a year previously, when I'd had to take cover inside, imagining that Penelope Quigwell was in league with my incredibly dodgy surveyor Charles Pimm. Back then, the shop owner had regarded me with knowing eyes. I remembered considering that look at the time, questioning it, wondering about his intentions. I'd expected him to challenge me, ask me what I was doing hiding among the grandfather clocks in his shop, but he had only offered a slight smile, a meaningful smile, then bowed and let me go on my way.

Although I'd never really analysed that moment —after all I'd been up to my neck in other concerns at the time—it had always remained in the back of my mind. It had obviously struck a chord.

"Doesn't it remind you of that room in the plan-odome?" Silvan asked. "Up there in the cosmos?"

I nodded. "It certainly bears a similarity."

He craned his neck to peer deeper into the rear, but it was difficult to see. The building was long and narrow, the shelves of clocks and freestanding time-pieces prevented us from getting a clear view down the other end. Somebody was in there, but we couldn't see whether it was our man or not.

"Shall we go in?" I asked and Silvan nodded.

I paused at the door, hesitating, then put my hand in my robes to pull out my wand. Silvan touched my arm lightly and stayed the intent. "No need to be all gung-ho. Let's tread gently, shall we?"

The bell above the door tinkled as I pushed it open, although how anyone would be able to hear it above the relentless ticking inside, I had no idea. The busy shop front was a tricky area to navigate, with items displayed on shelving in tall and narrow glass cabinets, or on pedestals. Baskets of keys and piles of cogs and springs otherwise littered the floor, too. We had to be careful where we were treading.

I moved sideways, wary of sending anything crashing to the ground, but also scared the proprietor would spy us coming and run out the back way. Assuming there *was* a back entrance and he hadn't already vacated the premises. I couldn't immediately see him.

As we rounded the final batch of display shelves, I spotted him. Dressed in a pink jumper with a banana yellow tie, and yellow chequered trousers, covered by grey robes that were open at the front, he made for an odd sight. His wavy sand colour hair was thinning on top, and he sported some kind of optical eye piece jammed into his orbital socket. Sitting at a battered desk, he was scrutinising the innards of a small pocket watch, prodding at them gently with a minute pair of tweezers.

"Just give me one second," he called, obviously more aware of our presence than it had appeared. We came up behind him and watched over his shoulder.

"Take all the time you need," Silvan replied cheerfully, stepping around me so he could take a closer look at what the man was doing.

We watched him work. He'd aged since 1983 of course. He had to be in his sixties now, but he looked well on it.

"Nearly done." A quick twiddle of the tweezers and the back of the pocket watch was clicked firmly closed. "There we are. Now what can I do for you?" He glanced up at us and for a brief moment looked puzzled. Then his face fell.

"How do you do?" he asked.

"We do very well, thank you." Silvan replied and reached forward to pluck the stop watch out of the man's hand to take a closer look at it.

"I've been expecting you," the little man said.

"I expect you have. I'm Silvan. This is Alfhild. As you know, we've all met before, but we didn't have enough time for formal introductions in 1983."

The man stood and shuffled towards us. "Paul Tiny," he offered, in a thin worried voice.

"Pleased to meet you, Paul." Silvan offered his free hand and Paul, uncertain as to what to do held his own out. Silvan shook it warmly.

"Do you recall where we met before?" I asked and Paul dropped his gaze to his feet.

"Yes ma'am," he said.

I nodded. "Would you care to explain what you were doing?"

"I—" Paul regarded us with uncertainty, probably wondering what our motives were.

"Only it would make things easier," Silvan chipped in, sneaking in behind Paul and perching on the man's desk. "I'm quite good at filling in the gaps, but Alfhild here has a rather overactive imagination. We should put her out of her misery, don't you think?"

Paul's shoulders crept closer to his ears. I had a feeling he badly wanted the floor to open up and swallow him.

"Please?" I prompted when I thought he would never speak up.

He took a shuddering in-breath. "I... I... I never planned what happened. I was staying at the hotel—"

"Whittle Inn," I reminded him.

"Yes. There. I was in my room and I located the very faint trace of a forcefield. I recognised that a binding spell had been used there and I was curious. It really all started as simple curiosity."

"Alfhild can understand that," Silvan said. "She's a pretty nosy individual herself."

Paul smiled at me uncertainly. "I started digging around. Scratched the plaster away and removed some of the wall below—it was just plaster and horsehair and small pieces of wood, nothing particularly solid. And that's when I saw what I was dealing with."

"You broke down the forcefield?" I asked.

Paul wrung his hands. "It's a simple spell really, once a forcefield has been revealed. It's quite easy to dismantle. If you don't know the forcefield is there you won't interfere with it."

"So, you broke down the wall and dismantled the forcefield, and then you removed something?" I prompted him again.

Paul stared at us, wincing in fear. "I wouldn't have taken it probably, but you guys turning up that way, at that moment... You startled me."

I wasn't buying it. I instinctively knew he'd gone straight for the Gimcrack.

"Which order do you belong to?" I asked. In all the time I'd been at the inn, nobody I knew had mentioned feeling or sensing a trace of anything in *The Throne Room*. How had this small, seemingly insignificant wizard been capable of locating the trace?

"The Grand Order of Timekeepers," Paul told

me readily enough, and justifiably with a certain amount of pride. The Grand Order of Timekeepers were well respected.

Silvan followed my train of thought, crossing his arms over his chest, still holding the pocket watch. "They're not known for sensitivity to defensive or secretive magick, are they?"

"No." Paul acknowledged this. "But my mother was an aura. I guess I inherited quite a few of her innate skills."

I whistled. I'd heard of auras but never come across one. They were a rare breed of witches who could sense even the slightest change in atmosphere or a movement or electrical current or pulse of energy. Little more than a will-o-the-wisp in human form, they were so highly-sensitive they only tended to live a short lifespan.

"She passed away when I was eight years old. My father was a lumberjack with the New Forest Order of Tree Witches, but he was an incredible craftsman too, and I wanted to be just like him. He didn't want me to follow him into arboriculture, he wanted me to better myself, so after attending the Celestial Academy I applied to several orders—"

"The Cosmic Order of Chronometric Wizards

by any chance?" Silvan asked and Paul nodded, his face glum.

"They turned me down."

"That can't have surprised you. They're one of the most secret of all orders," I said. "The toughest to get into I would have thought. But The Grand Order of Timekeepers? That's a pretty close second."

"Without the time travel though," Silvan mentioned casually. "That must have stung a bit. If that's what you were in to."

Paul looked between me and Silvan. "I didn't know what I'd found," he protested. "I liked the look of it. I was starting out in the business, and I was intrigued by anything that resembled a time piece."

"But you found out what it was?" I asked.

"Afterwards."

I didn't believe him. My instincts told me he was lying. "And?"

"It was a Gimcrack. One of the original ones I believe. An incredibly superior model. It would fetch a pretty penny on the black market."

"What did you do with it?" I asked.

Paul glanced around. "I broke it down. Some of the parts were quite valuable."

"Lies," Silvan said. "Do you believe him, Alf? Look, Paul, I wasn't born yesterday. If I knew something was valuable, I'd either keep it for myself or sell it on."

"So which did you do, Paul?" I asked, but he looked down at his shoes once more and refused to answer.

Silvan, like a dog with a bone, leaned forwards. "Do you do a bit of time travel, Paul?"

Paul cringed. "In this line of work, you get to know how to do it. I dabble a little. Just at weekends or in my spare time, you know?"

"You don't do it in the shop?" Silvan asked, and there was an air of menace in the words. Time travel would not go down well on Celestial Street. Maybe in Silvan's neighbourhood it might.

"Good gracious, no!"

"You don't take money from others who might want to time travel?" Silvan pressed the older man.

"Certainly not!"

Silvan clucked, his face a mask of disappointment. "Why are you lying to us, Paul?"

"I don't know what you mean," the little man protested, his face pale.

Silvan flipped open the back of the pocket watch. "Of course you do. The thing is, that by itself, a Gimcrack won't help you travel through time. It's just a glorified calendar, and nothing else.

Just like this little watch will tell the time and nothing else. There's nothing magick or special about this thing." He brandished the watch at Paul. "But with the Gimcrack, especially Gorde's Gimcrack, it was the magick inside that was powerful. The thing that fuels the Gimcrack. And whatever that is, it's not available to anyone—as far as I know—with the exception of the Cosmic Order of Chronometric Wizards." He stood and crowded Paul, "And they do not give up their secrets lightly, my friend."

It was my turn to be confused. "What do you mean?"

"I'm saying that Paul here recognised Gorde's Gimcrack for what it was. A machine with some magick inside it that could be harnessed for his own ends. Magickal essence maybe? I suspect that he's been indulging in time travel ever since. Not with the Gimcrack itself, but with whatever magick he found inside it." Silvan turned to Paul with a triumphant smile. "Am I right, Paul?"

Paul glared at Silvan momentarily, but his face rapidly crumpled.

"I get that this was a crime of opportunity," Silvan said, his tone kinder now, more conciliatory. "But Alf and I have to do what's right. We have to give what remains of Gorde's Gimcrack, and the magick inside, back to the true owners."

"Those Chronometric Wizards?" Paul asked.

I nodded. "It's their property after all. Well, I assume Guillaume Gorde would have left the Gimcrack to them."

"You have to know I didn't hurt that man," Paul said.

"We know. We've established that," I told him, feeling sad for Gwyn once more.

Paul scoured my face and nodded at me, his eyes knowing. "You hid in this shop once." He did remember, then?

"Yes. You saved me from a potentially nasty situation. Did you recognise me at the time?"

He nodded. "I thought maybe you had come for me then, but you didn't seem to know me. I have to admit I was relieved."

I laughed, breaking the tension. "Time travel is a peculiar thing. I didn't know you at all. Finding out about the missing Gimcrack, and meeting William Wylie, the wizard looking for it, that was still part of my future."

I reached out and patted his arm. "Listen," I said. "You did me a favour once, and I'm sure Silvan feels the same way I do. We can say you took the

Gimcrack by accident when you were startled. Let us have it back and we won't turn you in. I promise."

Paul hesitated. "What about the missing essence?"

"How much is missing?" I asked in alarm. How much time travelling had this little man undertaken?

"Not very much." Paul led us through to the back room, a store room of sorts. Here the shelves were laden with the teeniest and most intricate cogs, springs, tools, screws and pins I had ever seen. Right at the back of the store was a filthy parcel shelf. Dozens of dusty boxes were piled haphazardly on it. He reached to the back, and with practised ease withdrew a battered cardboard box.

Settling it down on a clear surface he carefully opened the box and slid out an object covered in a cream silk handkerchief. He gently unwrapped it, and Gorde's Gimcrack, entirely and unexpectedly in one piece, stared up at us. Although similar to all the other Gimcracks we'd seen, the exceptional quality was obvious. Crafted from hundreds and hundreds of tiny pieces of brass and gold, with quartz-headed pins, Gorde's Gimcrack, for all its cogs and springs, its internal workings on its outside, was an object of beauty.

"Oh," I breathed. "It's amazing."

"Yes. Yes it is," Paul agreed, handling it with reverence.

"The essence?" I asked.

Paul picked up the Gimcrack and pressed a hidden button on the side. Instantly the glass centre lit up, bathing the shadowy rear room in bright blue light. "It's inside," Paul explained. "You have to open it to extract any." He twisted the Gimcrack to the reverse, "And here, if you press this..."

"Whoa!" Silvan's hand shot out and extricated the palm-sized gadget from Paul's grasp. "I'll take that for safekeeping. Do you mind if I keep the box?" Without waiting for an answer, he carefully wrapped the Gimcrack in the handkerchief and slipped it inside the packaging before Paul could answer yay or nay.

Paul looked longingly at the box as Silvan tucked it under his arm. "That's a good job, well done," Silvan announced. "Thank you for your cooperation, Paul."

Paul, for the first time, examined Silvan with some suspicion. "And you will be giving it back to the Cosmic Order of Chronometric Wizards?" he asked.

"You have my word," I said hurriedly, before Silvan could come up with an alternative suggestion.

I held my hand out and Paul shook it. "We won't spill the beans, I promise."

We headed for the front of the shop, with Paul following us, a look of yearning on his face. "Pop in, the next time you're passing," he suggested.

"Oh, I'm never passing," said Silvan.

I shook my head at him in annoyance. "Well, I do. I visit Celestial Street quite frequently. I'll come and see you again next time I'm in London, Paul."

I waved and we walked away, heading down the cobbled street, for the rear entrance of the bookshop that would spit us back out into the mundane world. I could feel Paul's on us, watching us all the way.

As I stopped to scan my palm against the security screen, I glanced back. "If he's been using the essence to time travel, he's going to miss it, isn't he?"

Silvan grunted. "He'll have saved a secret stash of it, mark my words."

"He'll have drained some out and kept it, you mean?" That hadn't occurred to me. "Only someone as devious as you would think of that," I said. We entered the dark corridor and the security door closed behind us. I paused to let my eyes get used to the subdued light level. Silvan walked on ahead.

"Wait up," I called. "You'd better let me carry the Gimcrack."

Silvan picked up his pace and I had to break into a trot to catch up with him. The goddess only knew how much money magickal time-travelling essence would fetch on the black market, and I certainly wasn't in a rush to let Silvan find that out for himself.

CHAPTER SIXTEEN

Much later, Silvan and I arrived home in Whittlecombe. The train had been delayed and jam-packed with jolly, if slightly inebriated, football supporters who'd ventured to the capital to watch a big national match. Fortunately, we'd won, so everyone was in a good mood.

We hadn't really discussed how we could get Gorde's Gimcrack back to Mr Wylie, but by silent and mutual assent we had made our way straight to the clearing in Speckled Wood, arriving just before midnight. We sat on the benches there, kicking our heels, certain our cosmic friend would know to find us.

He didn't let us down. One second after the stroke of midnight, a bright blue flash alerted us to his arrival, and we stood to meet him.

"Good evening." He smiled happily. "You found it? I had a feeling that left to your own devices you would."

"We did." I brandished the box. "It's here. But where's my owl?"

Mr Wylie looked sheepish. "Ah. I believe I owe you an apology. I'd like to invite you to travel with me, for one last time. Maybe enjoy a spot of high tea... and erm... a little celebration."

"And if we don't, I won't get my owl back?" Surely, he wasn't blackmailing us?

I glanced at Silvan, unsure what to make of this development. He shrugged. The devil-may-care but Silvan didn't. He was always up for adventures.

"I promise you Mr Hoo has been well taken care of. In fact, he's even been enjoying himself. He seemed perfectly happy to stay on without you for a short while. Perhaps he understood you would be coming back for him." Mr Wylie lifted his Gimcrack. "Besides, I think we owe you the full story."

I nodded. "Alright then." I reached out to grab his arm. Silvan took the other side and once more we jumped through time and space. The sky and the stars swirled around us, the air rushed past my face and then we were back in My Wylie's planodome.

I hardly had a moment to catch my breath and Mr Wylie was whisking us through the door to the underground corridor. This time, when we clambered into the little buggy, we ventured left. It made no difference. The view from the buggy was much the same as before. White walls, lines of lights, nothing interesting to see.

"Where is Mr Hoo?" I asked, my stomach jittering with nerves. Mr Wylie had a nasty habit of keeping his own counsel and I wasn't fond of surprises.

"We're going to meet him now," Mr Wylie promised. "Nearly there. Just around the curve." We trundled on a little further. "Here we are."

Silvan and I dutifully followed Mr Wylie up a flight of tiled steps to an ornately carved wooden door in light wood. He tapped on it and stood back as it opened away from us, indicating we should enter ahead of him.

I stepped forwards and caught my breath. This was incredible. Spectacular. Unlike anything we had seen here previously. The domed ceiling sparkled with life. Much like a planetarium, the stars had been mapped out, and they winked at us from the deep blue skies. I could pick out comets, their long tails blazing behind them, and clusters of shooting stars. Whether they were Perseids or Geminids, or something else entirely, I had no real idea.

There were no telescopes here, nothing to indicate this was a laboratory, far from it. The lower part of the large dome looked like a theatre space, or a place of worship, or a court. There were rows of seating, like church pews, set on an incline so that everyone had a view into the bowl of the venue. Wizards in saffron robes were filing in from numerous doors and taking their places. The room filled with a hubbub of noise, murmurings, some laughter. I sensed the energy, the excitement. Something important was going to happen here.

In the centre of this circular space a large glass cylinder glowed with psychedelic light. It changed colour slowly, moving from one end of the spectrum to the other, incorporating every possible shade and hue in between. In the very centre of the tube I spotted a largish vial, approximately the size of a glass pint bottle.

"Essence?" Silvan asked Mr Wylie, who nodded and guided us over for a closer look. The vial was approximately three-quarters full of pale blue liquid.

"This, besides what is decanted into the Gimcracks, is all the magickal essence that exists in the entire universe. All that we've been able to find, that is." He lifted his own Gimcrack. "At any one time, only thirteen wizards are permitted to travel in time. They use their own individual Gimcrack, the one they created themselves as a novice. Each Gimcrack must be wrought by a wizard's own hand in our workshops during their apprenticeship. There are many, many levels to attain before anyone is entrusted enough to become part of the elite band of travellers."

"What happens to those who don't make it?" I asked, fascinated at this insight into Mr Wylie's world.

"They remain honourable members of the order. Every wizard who completes his or her training becomes a vital component of the operation. The measurement of time, the science and philosophy required to travel through space, the research necessary to understand the culture, history, communication, society and ideologies of the places we visit—these are all hugely important. There are others who monitor our travel and interactions, our wellbeing and so on. Everyone has a role to play."

Silvan peered closely at the essence. "How much of this is actually required to jump through time?"

Mr Wylie puffed his lips out. "Probably a thousandth of what you'd find on the head of a pin. It's powerful stuff. But the problem is... that it's finite. Once the essence has been used it can't be reused, so when its gone, that's it. It's more valuable to us than gold or diamonds or oil."

Perfectly understandable. "And that's why you needed Gorde's Gimcrack returned? To recover the essence."

"Yes. Gorde would have understood the importance of protecting the essence when he knew his life was failing. On one hand he would want us to recover the essence and on the other, he wouldn't have wanted to risk the possibility of a rogue time-traveller."

I thought guiltily of Paul Tiny, but Silvan and I had made a promise not to drop him in it. I had to hope Silvan was wrong, and that Paul hadn't saved much of the essence, if any at all. I avoided looking at Silvan and hoped my face wouldn't give the game away.

I held up the box containing Gorde's Gimcrack. "Then this belongs to you." Mr Wylie took it from me with care. He slipped the contraction out of the box and uncovered it, and I saw his eyes moisten as he gazed at the Gimcrack that had once belonged to his good friend.

"Thank you, Alfhild," he said. "And Silvan. You have greatly honoured the Cosmic Order of Chronometric Wizards with your assistance at this time. We will not forget."

He turned and beckoned, and a young wizard scurried forward. "Please return the contents to the source and properly cleanse the Gimcrack." The wizard nodded and rushed away.

"I must leave you now. For a short while. Someone will be along to show you to a seat." He nodded at us and disappeared through one of the side doors. I watched him go, then looked about.

The chattering and gaiety had reached a volume of epic proportions while we'd been discussing the essence, and now I observed the large numbers of Chronometric wizards gathering in the seats. I could hardly hear myself think. Whatever was about to happen here seemed to have put people in a good mood.

From across the dome I spotted someone waving at me. I blinked and screwed my eyes up to help me focus. Wizard Shadowmender? He appeared to be sitting among some other high-ranking officials, possibly the Council of Witches. I lifted my hand to wave back, just as Acting High Wizard Ballulah

Borodov joined us on the floor. I was relieved to see Mr Hoo perching on her wrist.

I reached out for him. "Hey!" I exclaimed, and with one leap he fluttered over to sit on my arm and rub his warm feathered face against my cheek. "Thank goodness you're alright!"

"It's time to take your seats," Ballulah said and indicated three in the front row. One for her, it turned out, and the others for Silvan and I. Mr Hoo took a perch on the edge of a wooden strut and twitted happily to himself.

"What's going on?" I asked Ballulah.

"This is the investiture of the new High Wizard. Now that we have Gorde's Gimcrack safely restored to us, and we know what happened to him, we can appoint someone new. Those are big boots to fill. Guillaume Gorde was an extraordinary wizard."

Silvan leaned forwards to speak across me. "I thought you were Acting High Wizard?"

"It was only a temporary post in my case. I'm an administrator by trade, not a time traveller. It was a great honour to serve in the interim."

I nodded. "So, who then?"

Around us the room hushed as the lights began to fade, and the excited murmurs ceased. There were a few shhh's. Ballulah nodded forwards where an old, old woman carrying a shining staff that stood taller than she, walked onto the floor, flanked by a pair of Chronometric wizards. I recognised the woman from pictures. Her long lustrous silver hair reached down to her calves and shone in the light. It took on the rainbow hue from the essence. Her face was at once ancient and yet her skin exuded health. But perhaps I might have known her through her charisma alone. The power of her magick radiated from her and bathed us all in its glory.

As one the audience stood. Even Silvan leapt straight to his feet. For this was Neamh, the Mother of Witches, and the leader of the Council of Witches. There was no greater living authority than she, and to be in her presence was an incredible honour for us all.

"Be seated, friends," she called, in a voice strong and pure. We shuffled into place once more. I held my breath and waited.

She lifted her staff and slammed it down on the hard-tiled floor. The noise reverberated through the dome. To my right, a single door opened casting a light into the darkened dome. Twelve hooded wizards, recognisable from their robes as the Cosmic

Order of Chronometric Wizards, slipped gracefully into the space and took their places in a circle.

Neamh turned slowly to take in all who had gathered here. When she smiled, it was a smile that enveloped us all, included us all in her love and joy. "Well met," she uttered, so quietly I should have strained to hear her, and yet it rang as clear as a bell in my head.

She turned back to the wizards in front of her. "Friends," she said again. "Today, we are gathered to witness a momentous occasion. We join here today for the selection of a new High Wizard." She indicated the glowing source of essence with her staff. "In a moment we will get to that. First," she turned again to address the audience, "let us take a moment to pay our humble respects to Guillaume Gorde, whose sad demise occasions this ceremony."

As one we climbed to our feet once more, this time bowing our heads. Neamh offered a simple but heartfelt memorial to Guillaume. "He was the noblest of wizards, an archetype of cosmic time travel, and a friend to many. He was loved and will be missed by all who knew him."

There were mutterings of agreement and we took a second to think of him and send love between the planes.

"While we're on our feet, I'd also like to offer our thanks to Acting High Wizard Ballulah Borodov for her generous support and fastidious organisation of matters to do with the Order while the investigation into Gorde's whereabouts was attended to."

There was a roar of approval and applause and Ballulah graciously smiled, lifting her hand to acknowledge it.

Neamh called our attention back. "Now to conduct the business in hand." She aimed her long staff at the glass cylinder. "Let the source of the essence choose the wizard who will lead the Order." Her staff spat a rod of white energy in the direction of the vial of magickal essence, and the room plunged into darkness. I heard the collective intake of breath, and then the essence lit up once more. Colours began to spin around the room—yellow, orange, red, purple, lilac, pink, blue, violet, green and so on—slowly at first, the gentlest of disco lights, then faster and faster until the world was a kaleidoscope of vibrant shades and I could hardly take them in. When I felt sure I would go blind the spinning abruptly halted and the room dimmed to black once more.

The next time the lights went up, they were directed at only one wizard. A man.

He blinked in shock and then began to beam. Once again, we took to our feet and clapped as hard as we could. The essence had spoken. The Mysterious Mr Wylie had been chosen as the new High Wizard of the Cosmic Order of Chronometric Wizards.

CHAPTER SEVENTEEN

The new High Wizard of the Cosmic Order of Chronometric Wizards waved us a fond farewell after the slap-up High Tea he'd promised. The cakes and sandwiches and sweet delicacies on offer were nice, but to be honest, Florence could have managed a better job of catering for the gathered throng of witches and wizards.

Star struck by some of the powerful personalities milling around the dome, I'd been a little sad to leave, but Silvan and I didn't really belong there. My place was at my wonky inn, Mr Hoo belonged with me, and Silvan well... wherever the devil he rocked up, I guess.

As we prepared to jump back through time, Mr Wylie stroked Mr Hoo's head and shook my hand. "Neamh wanted you to know she appreciated your efforts on our behalf," he said, and I blushed to think that she had even heard my name. The glow of pleasure began in my stomach and spread throughout my body. "Both of you." He nodded at Silvan, who for once, didn't quite know what to say.

"You'll have to tread a straight and narrow path from now on," I nudged him.

"It'll never happen," he replied, and part of me felt reassured by that.

We landed in the clearing. Midnight had come and gone but not by much. Time-travel is a wonderful thing when it allows you to party through the night and yet be home in time to manage a full night's sleep.

Mr Wylie turned to me and I recognised the small box he held out.

"Is this—"

"It's Gorde's Gimcrack, yes."

Taken aback I slipped the machine out and stared at it, in all its intricately crafted detail. Beautiful. "But—"

"It's been deactivated. I've had it properly and professionally cleaned. There's no trace of essence left inside. I thought you'd like it as a reminder of your adventure."

"That's really kind of you. It will be treasured."

Mr Wylie smiled. "That's all we can ask." He

lifted his own Gimcrack to make the final jump away.

"Wait!" I called. "What about Guillaume's body?"

"Can I entrust that to you, Alfhild? The Cosmic Order of Chronometric Wizards has no need of his remains."

I nodded. "Of course. We'll hold a private ceremony, right here in Speckled Wood."

"Perfect," Mr Wylie smiled. "He did so love it here." And then, in a flash of blue light, he had gone.

We burned Guillaume's remains on a miserable day a few weeks later. Wizard Shadowmender had agreed to hold the ceremony in Speckled Wood, and we used the clearing. In attendance were George—who had worked hard after my request to have the remains ceded to me—Silvan, Charity, Millicent, Mara cradling Orin, Mr Kephisto, Finbarr—keeping a close eye on his mischievous pixies—and Gwyn.

We made our memorial speeches and watched the fire burn down, eventually raking his ashes, and scattering them along the paths through the wood, heading back to the inn.

"He'd have appreciated that," Gwyn told me, the pain in her voice moving me to tears, not for the first time that day.

"He'll always be with us," I told her, and she apparated away. I expected her to disappear and I wouldn't see her for days on end but found her waiting for us when we returned to the inn. Florence and Monsieur Emietter had set up a feast in The Snug for everyone and we stood around nursing glasses of sparkling wine and tucking into miniature sandwiches with their crusts cut off, petit fours and madeleines, mille-feuille and angel wings, engaging in polite conversation between mouthfuls of sugary—and delicious—treats.

Eventually people began to drift away, back to their lives, as we do when we have lain someone to rest. For us at least, time continues to move on. Silvan however, remained slouched in one of the chairs in the bar, his long legs stretched out, his lips curving into a familiar smirk every time I looked his way.

I rolled my eyes and left him to it and went in search of Gwyn instead.

"Grandmama," I said, when I'd finally cornered her. "I have something for you." I'd left the box on the mantlepiece here in this room, waiting for the right moment to hand it over. I slipped the Gimcrack out of its coverings and showed it to her. "Mr Wylie gave it to me, but really I think it belongs to you. He was your friend after all."

Tears sprang into my great-grandmother's eyes. "Oh, Alfhild," she said. "I don't know what to say."

"Grandmama, you don't have to say anything. We can place it wherever you wish. Hang it on a wall or display it behind the bar." Gwyn nodded as I continued in a rush, wanting to get the words out before I lost my confidence. "I'm so proud of you and what you did all those years ago. You protected Guillaume just as he asked you to."

"You'd have done the same, Alfhild."

"Maybe," I shrugged. "Perhaps I'd have done the same because I share your DNA. I'm honoured to be your descendent, Grandmama."

Tears spilled down her face and she smiled. We reached for each other, and though I couldn't feel her physically, the hug enveloped my heart.

EPILOGUE

"Miss Alf! Miss Alf!"

Florence had been trying to get my attention most of the morning. This seemed unusual in itself because for weeks she'd been remarkably difficult to find whenever I'd needed her. Now here she was, dominating my line of vison.

I batted her and her feather duster away because Penelope Quigwell was demanding my accounts for the inn's VAT return.

"Not now, Florence, I am ridiculously busy!" As usual I was well behind with my admin.

And besides... Maths. Ugh!

"Miss Alf, please!" she beseeched me, and at last I looked up from my computer screen. She hovered in front of the desk, the feather duster beating away at the surface of the paperwork stowed in folders on top of my desk. Glittering as it scattered dust, it distracted me from Florence's eager face. I'd never noticed it do that before, but then given I wouldn't generally know one end of a feather duster from another, I'd probably never paid it much attention before.

"Miss Alf?"

I tore my gaze away from the feather duster. "Florence? What's up?" Her eyes were shining with excitement.

"I've had a letter, Miss Alf."

"A letter?"

"Yes." An envelope floated through the air and landed on my keyboard. It had been neatly addressed to Ms Alfhild Daemonne, c/o Whittle Inn, and it had been opened.

I narrowed my eyes. "This letter is addressed to *me*, Florence."

"Well yes, but..." she grimaced, her posture awkward.

I sighed, dreading to imagine what was coming my way now. "Spill the beans." There was no getting away from the fact that managing Whittle Inn meant there was always *something*.

"You see, Miss Alf. I heard that... erm... one of my favourite baking programmes—"

I groaned inwardly. "From Witchflix?"

"Yes, yes!"

"Go on." I rubbed my temples.

Florence practically jumped up and down. "They can't film where they normally film and they're looking for an alternative."

"Mmm?" *Oh dear. What a shame, never mind.* "What's that got to do with us?"

"Well I wrote to them. With the help of Miss Charity."

Oh really, Charity? "You pretended to be me? And you wrote to them?" I'd have words with Charity.

"And said they could film here."

I did a double take. "You did what? Film here? A TV programme? Florence, what were you thinking? Our kitchens would never be big enough. Plus we have the guests to think of... and... and Monsieur Emietter—"

The feather duster swiped at my papers knocking some of them to the floor. "No, no, Miss Alf. The producers will erect a marquee up in the grounds and all the baking takes place in there. It would be wonderful publicity for the inn!"

Her words halted the panicky thread of my thoughts. A marquee in the grounds with Whittle Inn behind it? She had a point there. Great exposure from a business point of view. And on Witchflix. *Hmmm.*

"And the producers actually want to come here?"

"They do!" Florence could barely contain herself. "According to the letter."

I pulled a sheet of paper from the envelope and began to unfold it. "Which programme?" I asked, grudgingly acknowledging her argument.

"*The Great Witchy Cake-Off.*"

Oh. I felt a sneaky frisson of excitement. All that cake.

"Okay." I scanned the letter. Favourable terms for us. And I had enjoyed what I'd seen of that particular baking programme. Harmless fun. What could possibly go wrong?

I thought about it for a moment, trying to imagine the negatives, but quickly decided it seemed worth pursuing. "Alright then." Florence hopped and skipped around in delight. "On one condition." My housekeeper paused, staring at me with a worried expression. "Until they get here, you're on your best behaviour and you keep house like you're supposed to. Deal?"

"Deal!" Florence twirled rapidly around, her

feather duster dancing with her. "Thank you, Miss Alf."

"You're welcome," I replied, distracted once more by the sparkling feather duster. Puzzled, I reached for it and it shimmied away from me. "Florence? Where did you get this feather duster from?" I asked.

She stopped dancing and the feather duster centred itself between us. This time when I tried to touch it, it remained in place. As my fingers made contact, I experienced a little current of energy. I'd always imagined the feather duster was controlled by Florence, using her kinetic energy the way a poltergeist will move things around a room. However, it seemed apparent this housecleaning implement had a magick all of its own.

"This old thing?" Florence asked. "Your great-grandmother gave it to me a long, long time ago."

"Did she indeed?" I stroked the fronds of the feathers and watched as they effervesced, then reached into the pocket of my robes for my wand. "*Revelare!*" I tapped my wand against the feather duster and revealed it for what it actually was.

The one item Guillaume had left with Gwyn, the tool she'd had to utilise in order to hide the Gimcrack because her own magick would not have been powerful enough by itself. The final piece of the puzzle.

Gorde's magick staff.

It had been hiding in plain sight all this time.

"Well I never." I smiled at my great-grandmother's ingenuity. "Well played, Gwyn. Well played."

PLEASE CONSIDER LEAVING A REVIEW?

If you have enjoyed reading *The Mysterious Mr Wylie*, please consider leaving me a review.

Reviews help to spread the word about my writing, which takes me a step closer to my dream of writing full time.

If you are kind enough to leave a review, you could also consider joining my Author Street Team on Facebook – Jeannie Wycherley's Fiendish Street Team. As it is a closed group you will need to let me know you left a review when you apply.

You can find my fiendish team at https://www.-facebook.com/groups/JeannieWycherleysFiends/

You'll have the chance to Beta read and get your hands-on advanced review eBook copies from time to time. I also appreciate your input when I need some help with covers, blurbs etc. We have a giggle.

Or sign up for my newsletter http://eepurl.-com/cN3Q6L to keep up to date with what I'm doing next!

The Great Witchy Cake Off

When a soggy bottom is the least of your worries...

The producers of Witchflix TV favourite The Great Witchy Cake Off are searching for somewhere new to base the filming of their next series, so Alfhild Daemonne invites them to Whittle Inn.

But what seemed like a great opportunity for a little harmless Wonky Inn self-promotion backfires when, at dawn on the first day of filming, one of the contestants is found toes-up outside the famous marquee.

Alf can't believe her rotten luck.

But it's not all bad news. The producers need a fresh contestant and Florence the ghost, Alf's long-dead housekeeper, is in the right place at the right time. Not so much to reap the benefits of instant fame and fortune you understand, because wouldn't that be nice? But more because she's an insider who quickly becomes party to all the gossip and the rumours.

Who knew the baking world could be so deadly? But never mind, solving this mystery should be a piece of cake.

Shouldn't it?

Chaos, catastrophe, ghosts and giggles in this warm and wonky clean and cozy witch series of mysteries.

The Great Witchy Cake Off is a standalone but complements the series as a whole.

Best served with a huge Devonshire Cream Tea!

THE WONKY STORY BEGINS...

The Wonkiest Witch: Wonky Inn Book 1

Alfhild Daemonne has inherited an inn.

And a dead body.

Estranged from her witch mother, and having committed to little in her thirty years, Alf surprises herself when she decides to start a new life.

She heads deep into the English countryside intent on making a success of the once popular inn. However, discovering the murder throws her a curve ball. Especially when she suspects dark magick.

Additionally, a less than warm welcome from several locals, persuades her that a variety of folk – of both the mortal and magickal persuasions – have it in for her.

The dilapidated inn presents a huge challenge for Alf. Uncertain who to trust, she considers calling time on the venture.

Should she pack her bags and head back to London?

Don't be daft.

Alf's magickal powers may be as wonky as the inn, but she's dead set on finding the murderer.

Once a witch always a witch, and this one is fighting back.

A clean and cozy witch mystery.

Take the opportunity to immerse yourself in this fantastic new witch mystery series, from the author of the award-winning novel, ***Crone***.

Grab Book 1 of the Wonky Inn series, ***The Wonkiest Witch,*** on Amazon now.

THE WONKY INN SERIES

The Wonkiest Witch: Wonky Inn Book 1
The Ghosts of Wonky Inn: Wonky Inn Book 2
Weird Wedding at Wonky Inn: Wonky Inn Book 3
Fearful Fortunes and Terrible Tarot: Wonky Inn Book 4
The Mystery of the Marsh Malaise: Wonky Inn Book 5
The Mysterious Mr Wylie: Wonky Inn Book 6
The Great Witchy Cake Off: Wonky Inn Book 7
The Witch Who Killed Christmas: Wonky Inn Christmas Special

Midnight Garden: The Extra Ordinary World Novella Series Book 1

Beyond the Veil

Crone

A Concerto for the Dead and Dying

Deadly Encounters: A collection of short stories

Keepers of the Flame: A love story

Non-Fiction

Losing my best Friend: Thoughtful support for those affected by dog bereavement or pet loss

Follow Jeannie Wycherley

Find out more at on the website www.jeanniewycherley.co.uk

You can tweet Jeannie

twitter.com/Thecushionlady

Or visit her on Facebook for her fiction www.
facebook.com/jeanniewycherley

Sign up for Jeannie's newsletter

eepurl.com/cN3Q6L

More Dark Fantasy from Jeannie Wycherley

Crone

A twisted tale of murder, magic and salvation.

Heather Keynes' teenage son died in a tragic car accident.

Or so she thinks.

However, deep in the countryside, an ancient evil has awoken ... intent on hunting local residents.

No-one is safe.

When Heather takes a closer look at a series of coincidental deaths, she is drawn reluctantly into the company of an odd group of elderly Guardians. Who are they, and what is their connection to the Great Oak?

Why do they believe only Heather can put an end to centuries of horror?

Most important of all, who is the mysterious old woman in the forest and what is it that feeds her anger?

When Heather determines the true cause of her son's death, she is hell-bent on vengeance. Determined to halt the march of the Crone once and for all, hatred becomes Heather's ultimate weapon and furies collide to devastating effect.

Crone – winner of a *Chill with a Book Readers' Award* (February 2018) and an *Indie B.R.A.G Medallion* (November 2017).

Praise for *Crone*

'A real page turner, hard to put down.'

'Stunningly atmospheric! Gothic & timeless set in the beautifully described Devon landscape .... Twists and turns, nothing predictable or disappointing.'

– Amazon reviewer

'Atmospheric, enthralling story-telling, and engaging characters'

– Amazon Reviewer

'Full of creepy, witchy goodness'

– The Grim Reader

'Wycherley has a talent for storytelling and a penchant for the macabre'

– Jaci Miller

Beyond the Veil

Upset the dead at your peril... Because the keepers of souls are not particularly forgiving.

Death is not the end. Although Detective Adam Chapple has always assumed it is.

When his ex-wife is killed, the boundaries between life and death, fantasy and reality, and truth and lies begin to dissolve. Adam's main suspect for the murder, insists that she's actually his star witness.

She claims she met the killer once before.

When she died.

As part of his investigation, Adam seeks out the help of self-proclaimed witch, Cassia Veysie who insists she can communicate with the dead. However, the situation rapidly deteriorates when a bungled séance rips open a gateway to a sinister world beyond the veil, and unquiet spirits are unleashed into the world.

Can Cassia and Adam find a way to shore up the breach in the veil and keep the demons at bay?

With time running out and a murderer on the loose, the nightmare is only just beginning ...

Praise for Beyond the Veil

'A 5-star winner from Queen of the Night Terrors'

– Amazon reviewer.

'Really got my heart pounding'

– Amazon reviewer.

‘A nerve racking, nail-biting, spine tingling, sweat producing, thrilling storyline that keeps you on a razor’s edge the entire tale’

– ARC reviewer.

‘Female Stephen King!’

– Amazon reviewer.

COMING SUMMER 2019

The Municipality of Lost Souls by Jeannie Wycherley

Described as a cross between Daphne Du Maurier's *Jamaica Inn*, and TV's *The Walking Dead*, but with ghosts instead of zombies, *The Municipality of Lost Souls* tells the story of Amelia Fliss and her cousin Agatha Wick.

In the otherwise quiet municipality of Durscombe, the inhabitants of the small seaside town harbour a deadly secret.

Amelia Fliss, wife of a wealthy merchant, is the lone voice who speaks out against the deadly practice of the wrecking and plundering of ships on the rocks in Lyme bay, but no-one appears to be listening to her.

As evil and malcontent spread like cholera throughout the community, and the locals point fingers and vow to take vengeance against outsiders, the dead take it upon themselves to end a barbaric tradition the living seem to lack the will to stop.

Set in Devon in the UK during the 1860s, *The Municipality of Lost Souls* is a Victorian Gothic ghost story, with characters who will leave their mark on you forever.

If you have previously enjoyed *Crone* or *Beyond the Veil*, you really don't want to miss this novel.

Sign up for my newsletter or join my Facebook group today.

Printed in Great Britain
by Amazon